# WEIRD HORROR MAGAZINE

SPRING 2024

## ISSUE 8

EDITED BY
**MICHAEL KELLY**

WEIRD HORROR 8
Spring 2024

PUBLISHER
Undertow Publications

EDITOR/LAYOUT
Michael Kelly

PROOFREADER
Carolyn Macdonell

OPINION
Simon Strantzas

COMMENTARY
Orrin Grey

BOOKS
Lysette Stevenson

ART
James Hutton

COVER DESIGN
Vince Haig

Weirdhorrormagazine.com

# CONTENTS

| | |
|---|---|
| ON HORROR<br>Simon Strantzas | 5 |
| GREY'S GROTESQUERIES<br>Orrin Grey | 9 |
| ALL THE THINGS WE NEVER SAID<br>Gary McMahon | 13 |
| CALCIUM<br>Jacob Steven Mohr | 21 |
| ON THE OCCASION OF A BLOODLETTING<br>RJ Taylor | 33 |
| ANY KIND OF FRIEND<br>Jack Klausner | 43 |
| ASTER<br>Elin Olausson | 47 |
| ECDYSIS<br>Jess Koch | 55 |
| RIGOR<br>Alison Moore | 65 |
| LONG SCISSORS, BLACK CANDLES<br>Perry Ruhland | 71 |
| PATIENCE IS THE VIRTUE<br>Aimee Ogden | 81 |
| HELLO<br>John Patrick Higgins | 89 |
| THE HAUNTING HOUSE<br>David Ebenbach | 105 |
| THE MACABRE READER<br>Lysette Stevenson | 113 |
| Contributors | 121 |

# ON HORROR
## SIMON STRANTZAS

## WHAT IS ANTI-HORROR?

AS A WRITER and editor of horror fiction, and as a columnist for this magazine, I spend an inordinate amount of time musing on what makes horror fiction work — not only on a plot and character level, but also on how language is used, and how pacing and atmosphere and implication and dread all work together to make a horror story cause frisson in the reader. The mechanics of horror fiction fascinate me as much as the narratives themselves.

    Recently, I've found myself intrigued by the idea of "anti-horror" — stories that intentionally take those trappings of and tools for telling a horror story and use them to subvert expectations and tell a decidedly non-horror tale. To help explain, let me first highlight the most important part of that description: the use of *intentionally*. By saying this is intentional, I'm excluding all those past non-genre works we have grandfathered into the Horror genre only because we recognize their themes or constructions have overlap. We claim these stories as horror while leaving unmentioned that the original writers did not have the genre in mind. For instance, is *Moby Dick* a horror story? There's certainly an argument for its inclusion under a broad umbrella. But Melville did not intentionally write Moby Dick as a horror story — at least not in the way we commonly define the genre now. Or what about the fiction of Cornell Woolrich, many of whose crime stories were written using the same tools as one might with horror — atmosphere, paranoia, dread? Those stories certainly read as horror or horror-adjacent, but the tools he used are not exclusive to horror fiction. They are tools that crime fiction and horror fiction *share*. His stories unintentionally overlap with horror. Because he lacked intent, his stories are outside the definition of anti-horror.

So if that's what anti-horror isn't, then what exactly *is* anti-horror? Anti-horror is a story that is told as one might tell a horror story — i.e., by using dread and atmosphere and a supernatural occurrence; by pacing with implicit suspense and using the same metaphorical language — but the objective of the story is not to solve the mystery of the occult or evoke a negative emotion such as fear. Instead, the anti-horror story subverts the whole notion of what horror is, telling a story focused on something else altogether. In essence, a story that *appears to be* a horror story without *being* a horror story.

Perhaps an example: Steven Millhauser's "A Haunted House Story" (found most recently in his collection *Disruptions*) involves a young man and his friends who dare one another to stay the night in a purportedly haunted house. The story takes great pains to setup the haunted house narrative, and to use the language of haunted house tales and the suspense they generate to provide the reader with the typical expected uneasiness. However the story eventually deviates and we realize the haunting, whether real or not, is not what the story is actually about. Millhauser isn't interested in the supernatural event at all, not even enough to explain it away. Instead, the haunting is there as the backdrop, revealing a different story, and thus defying the reader's expectation. Despite how it looks on the surface, in the end it wasn't a horror story at all.

This ambiguity about the nature of the supernatural plays a large role in anti-horror. While it's true ambiguity plays a role in horror itself as well, in the case of anti-horror it's not used to question the protagonist's reality or sanity. The ambiguity is not the point; it's simply another way to unmoor the reader and put them in a place where their expectations are distracted from the actual sub-narrative that's been going on beneath the surface of the story.

As I've said, I've recently been very interested in these stories — horror stories that aren't interested in horror — and how a writer might tell them. How a writer could use the tools of horror — the suspenseful language, the implications and paranoias and suspicions — and redeploy them to surprise the reader by taking them somewhere they weren't expecting. I wonder: can a story that seems to fall in the horror genre be satisfying if there is no moment of abjection or vastation? Will horror readers revolt if the payoff of an expected horror story reveals there was no horror at all? I'm not suggesting intentionally tricking the reader, but rather using the style and trappings of horror to take a story to an alternate non-horror conclusion.

The biggest challenge in finding an anti-horror story might be the market for them is likely small. They tend to fall into the trap of "too horror for lit fiction, but not horror enough for horror." This is especially the case with novels, but even with short stories where experimentation is more often accepted, the horror market hews toward fiction that identifies neatly in the category. Not necessarily trope-filled (though that often doesn't hurt) but recognizably horror, with story beats and a conclusion that fit reader expectations. The fear is readers will be disappointed if they don't get what they are used to. You may ask how true this is. Are readers really so resistant to something that doesn't fit firmly within the genre? I think, perhaps, on the whole, the answer is 'yes,' they are. It may be because people prefer something familiar, or because the familiar has trained people what to want, but either way, those editors and publishers who bring horror forward may not be willing to do the same for the anti-horror story. Or, at least, not with any regularity.

Which would be a shame, of course, but I suppose reasonable. If one makes their money selling horror, it's best if that horror is undeniable. Anti-horror, as an experiment with the form, will always be relegated to the exception and the special case. There's not a visible market for it in non-experimental settings. But that doesn't mean anti-horror isn't worth writing or reading. It's often these experiments that help us understand the mechanics and effects of the genre. Horror tools divorced from their expected effect can illuminate how and why the horror story can be so effective, and the subversion of the genre can clarify what our expectations are and allow us to reexamine them. Further clarity on the field is never a bad thing as it gives those of us interested in the genre a framework on which to expand and discuss why it is we value it to such a degree.

# GREY'S GROTESQUERIES
## ORRIN GREY

### FUNGUS OF TERROR: HOW FUNGAL HORROR GREW ON ME

AT THE TIME of this writing, it has been just over a decade since I co-edited my first anthology with Silvia Moreno-Garcia. *Fungi* was, as you can probably guess from the title, a collection of fungus-themed horror, science fiction, and fantasy tales from a bunch of extremely talented writers who we were very lucky to work with. It has done pretty well for itself since its initial publication, too, having been translated for release in Japan and, more recently, Brazil.

Silvia and I were already friends at that point, and she had previously published several of my stories, but my editorial duties came about because of our shared affection for a perhaps rather unlikely film, the 1963 tokusatsu horror flick *Matango*, which was released in the States as *Attack of the Mushroom People*.

*Matango* has an unusual pedigree. Helmed by Ishiro Honda, most famous as the director of the original *Godzilla*, *Matango* was released a year after Honda had directed *King Kong vs. Godzilla*, one year before *Mothra vs. Godzilla* and *Ghidorah, the Three-Headed Monster*. (There were also some other films in there; Honda was a busy guy.) Though the creatures from *Matango* are often lumped in with the various kaiju from those flicks, however, even appearing in the 1988 Nintendo game *Godzilla: Monster of Monsters*, they are not properly sized for city stomping.

Instead of a kaiju picture, *Matango* is an adaptation of William Hope Hodgson's seminal 1907 story, "The Voice in the Night." It's difficult, and often fruitless, to try to trace most horror tropes to a single starting point, but if fungal horror has one, then "The Voice in the Night" is it. The story tells of a couple stranded on a deserted island which is covered by a gray fungus. Driven by desperation, the castaways eventually eat the fungus and you can probably guess what happens next.

*Matango* is, in many ways, a surprisingly faithful adaptation, even though it adds a number of characters, and brings the entire enterprise to a modern (for 1963) milieu. The basics are still the same, however. The deserted island. The weird fungus. And the inevitable transformation into horrible fungus people. In this case, that means myconid-like humanoid mushrooms who make an absolutely unforgettable laughing sound.

Perhaps unsurprisingly, the rubber mushroom suits are the big selling point for *Matango*, but I love it unconditionally, for its sickly color palette, its eerie soundscape, and its inimitable juxtaposition of classic weird fiction and early color tokusatsu filmmaking — two great tastes that, as it turns out, taste great together. There are moments in *Matango*, such as when the survivor tells his story while looking out over the neon-lit Tokyo cityscape, that are as perfect a conjuration of the essence of weird fiction as any movie has ever managed.

I don't know precisely when my love affair with fungal horror first began growing on me, but it probably wasn't with *Matango*, and may not even have been "The Voice in the Night." A likely patient zero is the moldy corpse, an enemy in the 2006 Nintendo DS game *Castlevania: Portrait of Ruin*. According to the in-game bestiary, a moldy corpse is "a human consumed by evil after eating a cursed mushroom."

When first encountered, they look a lot like any other zombie — zombies, after all, being a relatively quotidian occurrence in a *Castlevania* game — but when you get too close, they convulse and drop to their hands and knees as huge, luridly-colored mushrooms suddenly sprout from their back and they begin to crawl toward you. It's a pretty great effect, and remains a high-water mark for fungal revenants, at least in my book.

And the years since *Matango* and "The Voice in the Night" — indeed, even just the decade that has elapsed since Silvia and I published *Fungi* — have seen no shortage of fungal revenants. Mycological horror has grown in popularity in the last ten years, thanks in no small part to video games like *The Last of Us*, which was adapted into a 2023 live-action HBO series.

While there are some fairly gnarly fungus-infected zombies in *The Last of Us*, many modern fungal horrors eschew the more mushroomy bad guys of something like *Matango* in favor of more bog-standard zombies who are simply infected with fungi, rather than a virus — see, for example, *The Girl with All the Gifts*, a 2014 novel by Mike Carey adapted into a 2016 film.

Naturally, the themes associated with fungus are part of the appeal of fungal horror for me. New life growing from decay; composite life-forms that are neither plant nor animal; the way that fictional fungi, at least, often draws elements from whatever it sinks its hyphae into, tying it into the sort of "radioactive evil" often presented in Lovecraft stories and perhaps best expressed in "The Colour Out of Space." (Lovecraft himself was no stranger to fungal horror, and incorporates it heavily into one of my favorite weird tales, "The Shunned House.")

At the same time, however, my reaction to these more recent fungal horrors tends to underscore that my interest in this genre niche is as much aesthetic as it is narrative. Put more simply, I'm never going to like a human-looking cordyceps zombie as much as I like the big, weird, laughing mushrooms of *Matango*.

Which is not to say that there aren't plenty of modern examples that still tickle my fungal fancy. In fact, as much as I love the mushroom people of *Matango*, my favorite fictional fungus monsters may be ones that only appear in the back matter of the 2006 Hellboy collection *Strange Places* — the same year as *Portrait of Ruin* and those moldy corpses; apparently 2006 was a good year for aficionados of fungus monsters.

While the Hellboy story "The Island" ultimately went in a very different direction, it was originally going to involve Hellboy washing up on the eponymous island, where he was going to be beset by fungal revenants. These remain almost exclusively in the

## GREY'S GROTESQUERIES

form of a handful of dialogue-free pages presented in the back of the collection. They've been inked and colored, but remain otherwise unfinished, and Mike Mignola claims that he can't remember what was going to happen next.

The revenants themselves represent an almost entirely distinct strain from either the more recent cordyceps zombies or the mushroom people of *Matango*, harkening back to the more amorphous descriptions presented in Hodgson's original story. "I thought of a sponge," the narrator of that tale says, describing his one glimpse of a fungus person, "a great, grey nodding sponge…"

The fungal monsters of the abandoned Hellboy tale resemble this, as much as they resemble anything else in the annals of fungal horror. They are blob-like shapes reminiscent of Gloop and Gleep from the old *Herculoids* cartoon series, complete with eyes that glow like their insides when Hellboy cuts into them with a saber discovered in the chest of a nearby skeleton. And as Hellboy lays into a horde of fungal revenants we see, through the cutaways which so characterize Mignola's genius, that each one is formed around the skeleton of a drowned sailor.

# ALL THE THINGS WE NEVER SAID

GARY MCMAHON

"WHAT THE HELL is that doing there?"

Anna followed me into the small living room, shutting the door with force behind her and taking off her coat as if she were wrestling with it. "What?"

We'd had a heavy night. The pubs in town had been rammed and there seemed to be a fistfight breaking out wherever we went. Too many drunken idiots; not enough joyful bonhomie. Your typical Saturday night in an English metropolis.

"That," I said, pointing at the coffin.

She dropped her coat on the floor and took a single step sideways, as if she were trying to get out of its direct line of sight. Her face was difficult to read: a strange expression, half shock, half smile.

"Is this a joke?" I took a deep breath, trying not to overreact, remembering what my therapist always said about breathing during times of stress.

"Not one of mine," she said. "Mine are funnier than this."

The coffin was standing upright against the wall. It was old and dirty; smears of dried mud decorated the wooden surface. The lid was open and propped to the side, leaning like a Saturday night drunk.

"I'm lost for words," I said, although clearly, I wasn't. "I mean, what the fuck are we meant to do with it?"

Anna approached the coffin. Slowly and cautiously. One arm held stiff at her side, the other one stretched out in front of her, hand open, fingers poised. She stopped just short of touching the coffin.

I shuffled my feet, then tried again to relax.

"At least it's empty," said Anna, not quite laughing but not quite *not* laughing either. "It could be worse. There could be a corpse to deal with." Then she did laugh; a short, sharp, rather ugly sound.

"Please," I said. "Don't even joke about it. You know how queasy I am about death." I looked around the room, half expecting to see a rotting cadaver propped up against the pillows on the two-seater sofa.

We walked across to the other side of the room, Anna flopping into the armchair and me standing in front of the television, fishing my phone out of my jeans pocket. "I'm calling Stan. He'll know something about this, I bet you."

Anna smiled, but it was an empty one: there was nothing of note behind her bared teeth. Idly, she reached for the television remote and switched on in the middle of a show — something about twenty-something idiots pretending to be marooned on a desert island with their exes. She kept looking over at the coffin, as if she expected it to have vanished.

Stan denied all knowledge of the coffin. At first, he thought I was having him on; it was only when I started to shout at him that he believed I was telling the truth. None of our friends knew anything. The whole damn thing was a mystery.

"Should we call the police?"

I shrugged. "And say what? There's no crime been committed. There aren't even any signs of a break-in. Whoever put that thing there, they gained entry without disturbing anything."

"Does anyone have a key?"

"Nope. You know me — too paranoid for anything like that."

"So what do we do?"

"I have no idea." I sat down opposite her, on the saggy old sofa. "I'm certainly not going to be able to sleep with a fucking coffin in the house."

"Are you scared it's owner might come back for it? Shambling along the street covered in grave dirt, bits of flesh and clothing dropping off its dry old bones?"

"Very funny." But it wasn't. It wasn't funny at all.

Eventually, we did go to bed. Anna was in the mood for lovemaking; I couldn't focus enough to become aroused because of that thing down there, leaning against the wall in the room directly beneath us.

"Come on...what is it they say about the proximity of death and people getting horny?"

Her lipstick was smudged like a scream. Her eye makeup looked like frontal head trauma. I turned onto my side, facing away from her. "Jesus, Anna. Get a grip."

"Is that an invitation?" She reached for me, digging her fingernails into my thigh; I pulled away, tugging the duvet around me.

"Stop it, Anna. I'm not in the mood."

I heard her sigh. The mattress shifted as she moved away from me, putting space between us. "Suit yourself," she muttered into the pillow.

It took me a long time, but eventually I drifted off into an uneasy sleep. Naturally, I dreamt about being trapped inside a small box.

When I woke, a slow-rising sun was shivering beyond the thin curtains, trying its best to illuminate another dull day. I noticed immediately that Anna was not in the bed. I reached out and felt her side: the mattress was cold.

Glancing at my bedside clock, I saw that it was 5:30 a.m. I'd not been awake this early in years — not since I used to work an early shift in a warehouse down the road.

"Fuck's sake, Anna..." I got out of bed, feeling worried but not knowing why. I slipped on a pair of jogging pants and an old T-shirt and left the room, headed downstairs. The lights were off. The day was only just beginning.

Anna was in the living room doorway, her body turned slightly so that she faced the coffin.

I stood behind her without touching her. The remnants of last night's argument were still hanging between us like old clothes on a line. "I was hoping that thing might be gone."

"No," she said, sounding faraway, as if she were speaking to me from another room, our voices separated by a partition wall.

"Come away from it. I don't like it."

She shook her head. Without seeming to have moved, she was now standing directly in front of the open coffin. She raised an arm, the hand opening.

"Come on. I'll make breakfast." My voice cracked halfway

through the sentence, like that of a teenager going through puberty. I cleared my throat. "Please, Anna...I'll do your favourite. French toast."

Her hand was moving. Closer to the coffin.

"It smells...musty. Like a house that hasn't been occupied for years. You know that smell? Flat and dusty and horrid." Finally, she touched the coffin. I knew she would. It was inevitable. "It's rough. The wood. Unfinished. I don't like it."

"Don't touch it, then, you arse. You might catch something." I was behind her, with only a short distance between us. I stared at the back of her head, the line of her shoulders as they visibly relaxed, her upper torso slumping.

Before I registered what was happening, Anna stepped forward, spun slowly around to face me, and kind of fell or stumbled backwards into the coffin. Her eyes were already closed. She looked asleep. Or drugged. Hollow cheeks. Pale skin. Hair as dry and wispy as cobwebs. She folded her arms across her chest in a stilted motion, the classic posture of a victim in repose.

"*It's comfy,*" she whispered without opening her eyes — or even moving her lips, as far as I could tell. I wasn't even sure if it was her voice — it sounded different somehow, like a faded analogue recording. "*Nice and old and comfy.*"

"Come out. Now." Panic gripped me but still I was unable to move. I simply couldn't bring myself to approach the coffin. No matter how hard I willed my legs to walk, they refused. The stubborn bastards.

The coffin door slammed shut. It was as sudden and shocking as a jump-cut in a horror movie: *slam!* She was gone...

"Anna..."

At last, I moved. Too late to matter. Just like always, my actions were too slow to make a difference, or to alter the course of events.

I went to the coffin and pulled at the lid, but it was stuck in place. I balled my hands into fists and hammered against the grubby, splintered timber. Forcing my fingertips between the lid and the casket, I tugged as hard as I could. There was a creaking noise — again, like a cheap horror movie sound effect — and the lid opened.

"Anna," I said again, quieter this time. But she wasn't inside.

All I could think of was that famous magic trick where the magician's assistant climbs inside of a box and disappears, only to emerge from somewhere else nearby — from behind a curtain, or through a trap door in the stage.

Biting back my screams, I did a trawl of the room, looking in every corner, behind each single piece of furniture. Absurdly, I even opened drawers and peered behind the standing lamp in the corner.

I found the second coffin under the sofa, with the dust bunnies and sweet wrappers that had slid under there to hide from the vacuum cleaner. This one was tiny, perhaps four inches long, two inches wide, and about an inch deep. Neat and shiny. Like a toy. Something you might get free in a cereal box back when I was a kid.

I sat down on the sofa and examined the small-scale coffin. Minutes passed; perhaps even hours; maybe up to a year. I couldn't be sure. Time was now an abstract concept. I fought the urge to laugh because it seemed inappropriate.

As the room began to darken, I grasped the coffin lid and forced it open. The creaking sound was a smaller, softer cousin to the one I'd heard before. The musty smell puffed out and into my face, making me blink.

She was inside. A tiny version of Anna. Resting on a bed of knotted pink satin, her arms crossed over her chest in the familiar pose. She was wearing a thin white dress: or was it a gossamer shroud? Gently, I traced the line of her jaw with the tip of my pinky finger. Her skin was cold yet rubbery, the cheeks coloured with rouge. I touched her hair. It was soft and glossy. This, I knew, was not a model, or a finely crafted figurine: it was Anna, in miniature.

"Please, baby…" I whispered. "Open your eyes. Open your eyes and see me."

She didn't move. Her eyes remained shut. I tried to move her arms, her legs, but they were rigid, as if *rigor mortis* had already set in. I thought about plucking her out of the coffin but I was terrified of breaking her. It took me a while to admit that there was nothing I could do.

Slowly, carefully, I closed the lid and secured the coffin inside my fist, staring at it as if the force of my will alone might make a difference.

When I finally looked up, glancing at the part of the wall where the full-size coffin had been, there was nothing there. Of course there wasn't. Perhaps there never had been. With any luck, this was all just a dream anyway and soon I'd wake up in bed next to her, my Anna.

### ALL THE THINGS WE NEVER SAID

I looked back down at my hand. My closed fist. I wasn't asleep. I was wide awake. More awake than I had ever been in my life. Regret filled me; I was sorry for so many things, even things I hadn't said or done. Real things and imaginary. Deeds committed by people I didn't even know.

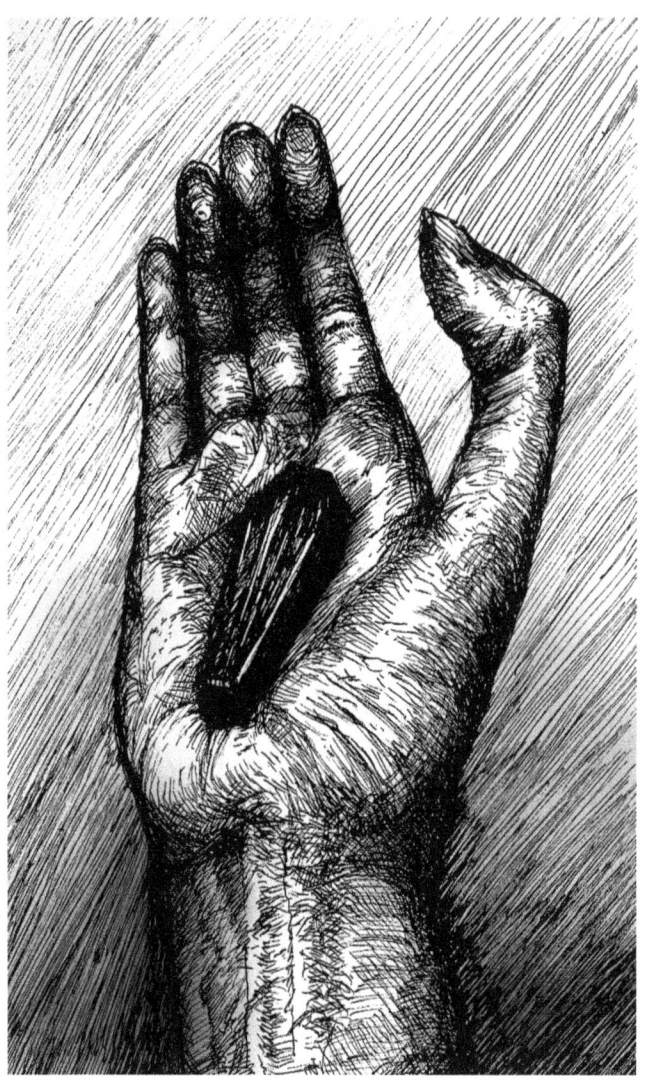

Anything and everything.
I was sorry for all of it.

I kept staring at my hand, inspecting the soft, light hairs along the back of my wrist, the scarred, whitened knuckles, the thin bones of my fingers beneath the papery skin, my ugly bitten fingernails. I should have said more, done more. There had been so much between Anna and me that was broken but might have been fixed, if we'd just sat down together and talked, like proper functioning human beings.

I'd stopped breathing. Had forgotten how to start again. My world lost focus and the walls began to close in. I felt, or sensed, something appearing close by, feeling certain that it was looming towards me.

I was terrified to open my fist in case this tiny coffin, too, had somehow vanished.

# *CALCIUM*

## JACOB STEVEN MOHR

CALEB — *if you're watching all this, if you're listening…*

My dad's opening my mail again. I come downstairs and it's on the Formica coffee table, arranged neatly like it's been filed there. Three envelopes, bellies slit open, their guts stacked beside them, still folded. Dear Old Dad's in the kitchen; he's doing the crossword, humming high up in his nose. He doesn't look up when I get to the living room, but I know he hears my bare foot on that one creaky stair at the bottom because his shoulders go tense, tight and huge across the back of that baby-blue button-down.

I scoop up the carnage and slither to the kitchen. Don't *say* anything — just hold the mail in my hand, angled toward him. I want him to know: that I *see* him, what he's doing, what he's *been* doing. Like rubbing a dog's nose in its own filth. But Dear Old Dad won't even cough. It's Saturday, but he's got a tie on anyhow. The solid red one, with the gold stripe right at the tip.

*You remember that tie, Caleb. You loved what we did with that tie.*

I break the silence. "Any packages come for me?"

Finally he turns, his expression like sanded wood. "Expecting something?"

"No," I lie. "Just checking."

"You got a package coming, I'll look out for it."

There's a shrug in his voice, but I hear craft beneath it. It's a game we're playing. His eyes glitter like dull crystals behind the mask of his glasses. His lips are a pale pink crease.

I rummage in the fridge, leaving Dear Old Dad to his 2-downs and 5-acrosses. One quick slug from the milk carton and I'm ready to slink back upstairs. I'm not hungry these days, not since the night in the park. But when I turn to go, I hear: "A little sausage left in the pan. I can reheat it for you." Somehow the thought of meat gets me salivating.

I scoop the links off the skillet barehanded, shovel them into my mouth cold. They're burned, caked with dried grease — they taste like cool early mornings. They taste like rushing out to meet the school bus. They taste like frost on weedy grass.

I eat six of them and wipe my mouth. "You opened my mail."

It's an easy serve. Dear Old Dad slaps it down without effort: "My mistake. I'll do better."

Then I'm heading back upstairs, finding the squeaking step at the bottom and grinding it under the ball of my foot until it shrieks. The sheen of the gold stripe on Dear Old Dad's tie catches the light as I ascend, like a gold tooth in the back of a smile.

I wave away your whispers, your urgent accusations.

You *loved* what I did to you with that tie.

꩜

The boxes started coming middle of June — one week after Cabrini Park. And you managed it so *cleverly*, Caleb, right from the beginning. Nondescript brown parcels, packing peanuts brimming inside, just enough of a scribble on the return label that it looks like somebody tried.

But you *always* did this so dexterously. Secrets, subterfuge. I can't pretend I'm surprised.

Wednesday — the first delivery's up on the townhouse stoop when I get off work at the butcher shop, in that small hour of solitude I get before Dear Old Dad drives up from his office job. I kick it with a toe: it rattles, a muffled Styrofoam-y sound. It's as big as a carry-on suitcase, just big enough to fill my arms when I haul it inside.

Already I know better than to open it at the kitchen table. Up the stairs, on the bed with a *whumf* sound — it's not heavy, but its weight still presses a dent in the mattress. My keys tear packing tape away in thin curling strips until the box (the gift, *your* gift) opens up like a bloom. Then I'm rooting blindly in the Styrofoam peanuts until my fingernails scrape something rough and solid.

I wrap my hand around a long rigid shaft; I pull…

A femur. A *man's* femur. Picked clean, bleached sugar-white. 100% human.

I dump the box, do inventory. One femur plus three bones in the right foot, two vertebrae, four ribs, and one guitar pick-shaped kneecap. They lay in a rough semicircle: *Can you complete this picture?* But none of the pieces connect. The foot-bones rattle in my hand like dice when I scoop them up. I fidget them, rub them together — their texture catches on the calluses at the base of each finger. Somehow the grisly truth of what I'm holding eludes me. They aren't a *skeleton*, after all. Not a framework for muscle and skin and organs and yards and yards of capillaries.

They aren't pieces of a human. They are only themselves; they are only bones.

Dear Old Dad's key, struggling with the lock downstairs. I shove the bones back in their box, scrape the packing peanuts off the floor and pile them on top. Then the whole thing's crammed in the bottom of my closet, covered by dirty clothes, and the door's shut tight. And yes, I can hear you already, Caleb. Your whisper tickling the hairs above my ears: not words yet but just your shuddering breath, just on the edge of un-control. The end of one thing — the start of another. But when Dear Old Dad's heavy footsteps stop at my door, my heart rate doesn't flicker.

Why should it? I wrestle a laugh. There's no skeletons in my closet. *Not yet, not quite.*

∼

Think about hostage situations, Caleb. Deadlocks, logjams. Dear Old Dad, fingering through my junk mail, my garbage; peering at my laptop when an alert ghosts across the screen. Being so fucking *attentive*. I swear he's been on my laptop, even though I bring it with me whenever I leave the house, even though I scramble the password once a week.

I pretend to care. So he feels *engaged*, so he looks where I want him looking.

## CALCIUM

It was the pig who started it. This is him: barrel-chested and corn-fed tall, like a cartoon cop should look, leaning on the railing of the stoop when I open the door — like he's been there the whole fucking time. Uniform blue as the sky. His smile's tight and practiced, but my eyes drift again and again to the metal heft of his gun. I'm always flabbergasted at just how high they wear them, their pieces, how obvious they are, nestled snug against thick pig stomachs.

He says, "I'm looking for Eddie Rafferty. He in now?"

"That's my dad," I tell him. When the cop talks, I count all of his teeth, like he's a ventriloquist's dummy with a loose-hinge jaw. "He's at work."

"Oh — sorry." The cop looks down like he's consulting a clipboard, but there's nothing in his hands; the big fake smile doesn't drop a centimeter. "I meant, Eddie Junior. That's you?"

I shrug. A *bright* pig — I try not to show the jolt on my face. "Sure. Okay."

From there, it's all the questions I'd rehearsed for. About that week in June. About you. When had I seen you last, where were we, what were we doing, who else was there. What was our *relationship* to each other. You'd have been relieved, Caleb — at how easily the lie flows off my tongue. *School friends, teammates.* Nothing salacious to get his pig blood pumping.

Nothing of the truth, nothing of the real you, the real me.

He doesn't write any of it down. I picture him in the cruiser later, mumbling into a tape recorder or scribbling notes in a spiral-bound book, too tiny for his farm-raised paws. After it's all done, he whips a card from his chest pocket, waggles it under my nose.

"If you think of anything else, Eddie Junior. I'll be in touch."

He's searching my face, looking for whatever guilt looks like on a face. But I'm thinking beautiful thoughts. How the late sun poured over the sloping dam wall. The cool dark gray of the lake's flashing surface. The red tie, almost purple in the deepening twilight.

I take the card, smile so wide my cheeks hurt. "I just hope he's all right."

Surely he'll leave then, but no: he lingers, just watching me. My nerves scream to sink back into the house, into the comfort of behind-closed-doors. But I won't retreat. I let him stare into me, even though the sun's behind him, pinging off car windshields in the parking lot and knifing my eyes. I hold ground. Then he asks me one more thing.

"Caleb — he seeing anybody? A *girlfriend* we should talk to?"

That's when Dear Old Dad comes up the walk.

I don't know what he sees on my face, what he *thinks* he sees. But our eyes lock and there's a hint of light in his, some animal intelligence I've never spotted there before. The cop leaves without an answer, lifting his chin as Dear Old Dad waddles past. And I'm up in my room, music turned way up, lights turned way down.

The sullen hormonal teen: I slip it on like a Halloween costume.

I ignore his first knock, and the second. But I *know* — this new paradigm, this top-to-bottom reorganization of the world — it won't be ignored. And when the intrusions start: the snooping, the sudden interest in my daily banal thoughts, my fucking *feelings*, I know. He's a dog with a rawhide bone, my Dear Old Dad. And he'll chew and chew until he's chewed my whole life to bits.

He won't ask the question. He doesn't talk about you; he wouldn't dare. So it's a staring contest we pretend we're not having. A comfortable stalemate — for a while. But bath water grows cold, coma patients get bed sores. Anything can become intolerable, even a loving father who just wants to know how you're doing. Even stalemates suppurate if you wait long enough.

But *we* don't have to wait. We figured it out — how to bust a stalemate wide open.

*Didn't we, Caleb?*

In my mind, it's still June. Still dead-dog summer. But the cop got his dates wrong. Late May was the last time anybody really saw you, Caleb. That night in the park, you were already gone.

I hear you before I see you. Coming up the long stone steps, cresting the dam wall; I catch your sneakers scraping the greenway cement under the scream of cicadas. Then you're there: awash in muddy yellow streetlight, waving mosquitos out of your face. I swear you never looked better than that. Just a distant uncertain shape, almost glowing, almost heavenly, not seeing me, never really seeing me. "Ed? You here?" You look right and left, like a kid crossing the street. Then, completely oblivious, you start slowly towards me, along the dam.

I'm thinking about that last text again, Caleb. But really, I'm

## CALCIUM

thinking about the spaces in between your texts, in between calls, late-night encounters. Time engorging, filling empty nothing with itself. Forcing me to plug gaps I never agreed to fill. I tried returning space for space. But by the time I read *I want to talk face to face*, there was nothing left worth saying.

I texted back, *Saturday Midnight Cabrini Park*, my mind already made up solid.

And now you're closer, so close I can see you sweat and hear you breathe. Even in the dark it's too hot; under the hot park lights, your face glistens like the surface of the lake a dozen yards below us. Beads of perspiration marble your cheeks. Here in hiding, my underarms and ass crack are swamps. The bugs are maddening. But I lie still. I let you come.

Because listening to you breathe — nervous and flighty like you've got precognition, like you've seen this all happen before — I can tell already what you want to say. They won't be your words. They'll be your Mommy Dearest's, *your* Dear Old Dad's. They'll come from Counselor Rick at school, or your fucking *priest*. Or Lorie, on swim team, who thinks I don't see her ass-glancing when you heave out of the shallow end after the hundred butterfly, slick and shimmering.

I know what words they slipped between your lips. I've got my answer ready.

You pause — so close I could reach out, unknot the laces on your sneakers. Your breath catches; you're a deer scenting the air. "Eddie?" you whisper — to nothing, to nobody.

Your phone, clutched in one clammy hand, goes up to your ear. I don't know who you were going to call. It doesn't matter who. I'm rising up out of the grass; my blood is ocean waves in my ears, between the echoing walls of my skull. You're turning toward me, slack-jawed, *and the red tie is in my hand, and you're kissing it now, sucking it now, choking on it, gagging for it…*

You love it. You love me. Not the first time, and not the last.

～

Clattering, in my closet, in the cramp of darkness. The muffled jangle of cardboard and long bones. It shakes the bifold door on its rolling track.

I *knew* the gifts were yours. I always knew. You were never hard to read.

After July, the deliveries are biweekly. Small or large, heavy or light, long and skinny or bread-box squarish. Always full of bones. Your bones. You gift me your tibias, your scapulas, your metatarsals. I assemble a xylophone of ribs, the minute machinery of your inner ears. You send your slack lower jaw, shorn of teeth; then, next week, a box with a baggie full of clicking yellow molars. When your upper skull shows up four days later, I join it with its mandible, fitting your teeth into their grooves like pieces of a jigsaw.

Your face reformed, I press your bared grin to my lips.

I take you back. I accept your apology.

When people say, *sins of the flesh,* they mean *meat.* Soft tissue. Skin, tongues, genitals. We discover, together, the unyielding sensuality of bone. Now I sleep with a long, tapering fibula beneath my pillow. I knit your right-hand bones together; I know their grip, gentle or demanding, across every inch of myself. Your skull leers from its shelf in the closet, gleefully watching.

No eyelids — you can't take your eyes off me.

I've started folding my shirts to stow in dresser drawers. The boxes fill my closet, piled teeteringly high. Sometimes I consider consolidating. Picking one big package, filling it with all the pieces of you, crushing down the rest and hucking them in the basement behind the furnace. But I resist temptation. Every night, I hear that *clack-clack-clack* like wind chimes. I don't think in numbers of bones anymore: I think of protein, collagen, minerals. I think in ounces of calcium. I think of my father taking bolt cutters to the bike lock on the closet door, you spilling out in pieces like dice across the floor. Or, not in pieces at all. You, standing just on the other side of that door, not with a skeleton's grin but a blank all-tooth sneer.

I know your gift is an apology, Caleb. But your whispers still accuse me, still molest me, still point bony fingers while your real finger bones snap and tumble in a shoebox. I ignore them — unless I want your hot breath on my shoulder. We don't need to talk. Our relationship is completely physical now. See-through and open. It's enough. It's what we *want.*

From that grin, I'd say we've never been happier.

**CALCIUM**

Then I come home from work and my bedroom door's off its hinges.

Dear Old Dad. He knows — *thinks* he knows. It doesn't matter which.

He's squatting near the open doorframe, showing ass crack to the landing and stairs. His toolbox yawns behind him, jaw unjointed. His fingers are black with grease to the knuckle. The door's leaning against the wall by the bathroom. My bedroom light is on, the ceiling fan twirling.

The closet door is just cracked, in spite of the lock.

"What the fuck is this?"

Dear Old Dad heard me come up, but he won't turn to look. "Don't swear, Eddie Junior."

"My door's gone." My face feels stretched tight, flat on my skull.

"Good eye." He forces a smile like we're sharing a fucking *joke*. "Give me a hand?"

I stare at him until he meets my gaze: his face is steak-pink with exertion, but there's a deeper kind of fatigue underneath the glare of his work goggles. "It's been rattling in the frame."

A lie — when did he get so good at lying? "Bullshit." But maybe it's not.

"Thought I'd resettle it on the hinges, but it's worse than I figured. Might have to reframe the whole thing to get it hanging right in the end. Could be a big job."

I work a little cheek-flesh between my top and bottom rows of teeth. "How long?"

"We can talk about that." Dear Old Dad heaves to his feet. I remember him taller than me, but despite his bulk he seems shrunken, diminished. *Skeletal*. "You want to talk?"

"I'm busy." But it's like all the heat's been sucked out of my lungs. I brush past him into the room, but without the door, there's no finality to it. I'm a raw nerve end now. I'm exposed. Dear Old Dad stares at me through the doorway. He's an old man, hardly even there.

"I'm thinking burgers for dinner." He hefts his tools and lumbers away.

I flop back on the bed, glaring at the fan, my energy spent. Round and around the world spins. I can hear Dear Old Dad's boots treading down the stairs, avoiding the creaky step at the bottom but still waking the dead. I hear his grunting breaths, his heavy hand on the rail. Then nothing.

I don't know how long I lie there before that last box catches my eye. Low and flat, like the very first, lying by the far corner of the closet door. I spring up from the mattress: the packing tape's torn cleanly, with a kitchen knife or box cutter, the cardboard flaps hanging slightly open.

But the contents are undisturbed.

I'm not breathing. I'm prying the flaps apart, scattering Styrofoam like flower petals. And it — *you*, the last sculpted *piece* of you — seems to catapult into my hand. It's even already assembled: your *pelvis*, Caleb. Hipbones and coccyx and tailbone, heavy in my hands, and so warm, almost throbbing. And suddenly the closet door is thundering, wheel-track loose and rattling, shaking to pieces like your fists are *smashing* against it from inside…

*You whisper.* I lean back into you, shuddering. Your embrace is rigid, adamant. Your arms wrap around my shoulders: humeri, radii, ulna. Lipless jaws scrape my cheek. Ribs invade my spine. You shouldn't be standing — your hips, your center, all still clutched in my hands. But your voice, whistling between unmoving teeth, reminds me not to think of numbers of bones.

Think instead of transformation. Of renovation, of climax.

Dear Old Dad calls up the stairs. "You coming down, Eddie Junior?"

*The end of one thing — the start of another.*

∼

*Caleb. If you can hear me. If you were ever really here.*

We're creeping down on sock feet. Your fingers dig under my collarbone; your infernal breath moves the small hairs on my neck. We're one entity now: skin across muscle across bone. Our hips brush the railing, our feet miss that one creaking stair before the bottom.

Dear Old Dad, in the kitchen again. Everything repeats. "You hungry?" he asks, without turning.

We're behind him in the den, slinking forward in exaggerated tiptoe.

He shouldn't hear us — we're so quiet, so insubstantial our feet don't even touch the vinyl plank floor. But he does. Because his shoulders go tight across the back under his wife-beater, under the tight pale skin. His work goggles perch on his head; I imagine them filmed with sweat on the inside, the lenses frosted. He turns, not enough, like a dog cocking its head.

"You wanna talk now. I guess we could do that. I guess that's…"

He loses steam, deflates. Like you did. On the table stands a cup of milk, half-drunk. His fingers flutter but don't touch it. Even the glass is sweating in this heat.

"I never said nothing. About you and… Even when they came to the office. The cops."

You press into me from behind. Your ribs yawn wide, puncturing my flanks, sliding beneath the skin. Now that rattle, that clack-clack-clack, quivers inside me. You stretch me from within, filling me out, forcing me forward — like there was a choice before, like I ever had a choice.

"You're my son," he insists. "My son. No matter what."

Your pelvis, heavy and sharp in my hands. Heavier than it looks. Twenty-two pounds of bone in all. The sacrum. The pubic arch. The narrow blade of the coccyx, pointed down at his bent-forward neck. Protein, collagen, minerals. Calcium.

"I love you." But it's a whisper. Maybe I don't even hear. "You know I…"

I do. And if he'd turned, if he'd just looked at me, it might have been different.

∽

Then the room's just us. No telling where your bones stop and mine start. You're in me, pressed up *against* me. Your chin digs against the hollow of my neck; I'm fishing in my pocket, finding that little blue card that's got the pig's name and serial number. I feel your jaw hinge open — I feed the cardboard between your teeth, listening as you chew it to pulp.

The end of one thing. The start of another.

*And another, and another...*

Fiber coats my tongue. Nobody would ever believe it anyway.

# ON THE OCCASION OF A BLOODLETTING

## RJ TAYLOR

THE PLAGUE DOCTOR'S clock cries out the hour.

Under its bell jar, the trapped machine twists its gears and the fated time of his departure grinds irreversibly into place.

The doctor stands. Ten arms tall, masked and robed, he is imposing even unto demons. This is part of what makes him a good doctor, able to frighten the plague from its haunting places. But it is neither demons nor plagues he faces now. It is plucking down the last rotten fruit, pulling off the last squirming, blood-bloated leech; it is his final deed to complete before he can leave this filthy city.

He has seen visions of his future. Twisted trees and crumbling mountain paths. Shadows of desire for too long now. He will continue on, his unnaturally long life leading him to new horrors. But he can take nothing with him, and he can leave nothing behind.

His robe falls pupil-black, slick and complete around him, settling from his abrupt motion as easily as death settles upon a body. He must face what he has let run wild too long. And then he must go.

The eyes of the paintings beside his desk open in surprise and watch him as he slips his meticulous ledger in beside vials, and snaps closed the clasp of his medicine bag. They stare unblinking as he lifts the bag.

The paintings, whatever their thoughts, cannot scream out in either fear or fury, but can only watch silently as he walks out.

## ON THE OCCASION OF A BLOODLETTING

Across the city, through a spiderweb of dark streets, the Madame sits at her desk listening to the echo of her own intricate, ornate timepiece screaming out the hour.

She too keeps a ledger of numbers and she too tracks the decline of bodies, her own impervious to the ravages of time. The eyes of her paintings are lidded with exhaustion, red-rimmed from the things they have seen. Her raven, though, blinks curious, ever alert as it hops and flutters from her shoulder to her desk.

The Madame, in her tailored vest and crisp white shirt, watches the door to her office. Her own eyes are kohl-lined, glazed, waiting.

He will come, at least, to say goodbye.

The doctor stalks the city streets, robe billowing in drafts of putrid air. Vermin scurry along gutters and everywhere a thick miasma rises to the starless sky. The doctor's mask, maggot white against the darkness, is stuffed with camphor cloth, but the reek of rotted flesh is inescapable. Such a familiar perfume.

He has been in the city long enough to move by intuition, though still a stranger. It is this way everywhere he visits. And everywhere there is always another lover to leave behind. He is used to cruelty. Though this time there hangs a loose thread, like the lingering moan of the dead. One last deed before he can leave. He turns a corner and past a wall of red weeds so thick they reach for him, twisting as if in agony as they stretch their tendrils towards him.

As he walks, he wonders at his affections, his history. His time with the Madame was delicious, like rare meat in his starving mouth. Not love. He wonders if he is capable of love. But the wondering is just thought-play, the way one might absently consider how loudly the city would scream if one were to add torch-fire to the methane-soaked wood piles. Idle considerations.

He takes another corner, around past the dull-eyed man always plucking the feathers from an endless pile of dead ravens, their newly naked bodies stacked like pastries at a banquet. The doctor slows. He is close to where he suspects, where he fears, he will find his prey.

He cannot go to the Madame emptyhanded. No. She must face

the ragged remains of their affections, as he is. He pulls a spindly, twitching mechanical device from his robe and holds it in one gloved hand while he twists its gears with the other. When he's satisfied, he sets it down onto the soot-strewn street. It shudders for a moment, then skitters away, the doctor's boots pounding close behind.

## ON THE OCCASION OF A BLOODLETTING

The device runs out the narrow roads onto the boulevard. It is deserted at this hour, but the granite gray statues glower down, dwarfing even the doctor as he follows past the shuttered mansions and the ornate fountain running rust red water.

The device turns down a side street indistinguishable from the others and the doctor hurries after. A wind howls down the boulevard, bending the burnt-black trees and forcing the doctor to slow. He holds his bag against his chest, one hand on his hat, until he can duck down the street, just in time to see the silver glint of the device as it disappears around another bend.

Even with his long legs, the doctor must move quickly to keep up. But there is only one more corner and then the device locks its spindly legs into a skidding halt, its joints clamping stiff as if in terror. It has found his prey. The skid ends at the edge of a rag heap. The doctor starts down the alley after it but slows, his robes swaying like heavy drapes jerked shut against some midnight monster.

Along the alley, past the shuddering device, atop the heap of torn clothes, a child as white as a red-eyed rat kneels, its back to the doctor. It is pawing through the rags, senseless to its observers.

The doctor watches, breathing camphor, waiting. After a moment he sets down his bag, undoes its clasp, muffling the click beneath his thick leather gloves. From the bag's innards he pulls a hook, glittering zinc and heavy. The kind that clicks closed, strong enough to secure a heavy, struggling burden. The kind used by seamen, by butchers.

He glances at the child. It continues to dig at scraps. The doctor allows the hook's heft to slip into his palm, his gloved fingers to curl around its sides, a fist to form around the metal, the curve jutting out fierce and ready.

Across the alley the spindly device stutters and chirps. An innocent act of mechanical logic.

The child starts, then arches its back, the shadows of tiny vertebrae visible beneath its threadbare shirt. It stands motionless for a moment, a small creature under the fearsome darkness around it.

The doctor matches its stillness. But he feels acutely the pulsing of his own blood, the meat of his own body. Breath comes and goes and comes, and for a moment the doctor thinks he is choking, finally suffocating on the herbs in his mask. But no. The sound comes from the child. Breath, breath, breath. Is it crying? Is that possible? Its tiny ribs heave. Its tiny shoulders rise and fall.

No. The doctor closes his fist tighter on the hook. The child is not crying. It is sniffing the air.

Like a beast.

The child turns. Even in the darkness its eyes gleam lid to lid pure red. Its lips, white as the rest of it, peel back into a hiss and its entire little body twitches like the limbs of a bug crushed beneath a fist.

The doctor steps back, his boot sinking into some unknown sludge. He ignores it, ignores all but the red eyes of the child. Not breaking gaze, he crouches low.

Under his breath he whispers *ad tata*, the imperative reaching only the end of his mask's beak, but the reminder of its reality giving him the reason to fight. He does not wait for the child to obey but steps forward.

*Ad tata.* Come to father.

The child remains still, but screams. An undulating animal howl. The doctor takes another step and the child shutters into itself, a crouch. Clicking the hook, the doctor advances, steps now steady, confidence only half-feigned.

He's nearly within reach when the child springs, shrieking through the air so fast the doctor has no time to dodge and only by mindless impulse does he twitch far enough aside. The child wails, clinging on to the cracks in the far wall, suspended out of reach above the doctor, scraps of rag fluttering down from it like dead leaves.

The doctor clicks the hook open and steps back ahead of the child's attack this time, letting the child drop like a weight down where he'd been standing. But after such a fall it isn't stunned even for a moment and when the doctor lunges for it with the hook, the child darts to the far wall, back over the doctor's head and then again against the wall high above. It crawls up the wall, red eyes thick with hatred, watching the doctor. It could stay there, out of his reach forever. He needs to tempt it back down.

*Ad tata*, he says again, louder. A weak incantation, an imperative. But more than that — truth. Truth is always the greatest mockery.

The child doesn't scream, but springs so fast from wall to wall that the doctor can't track it; and from a direction he isn't even sure exists in this world he feels the impact of a small, heavy body crashing against his robes.

## ON THE OCCASION OF A BLOODLETTING

And following that, the dark rush of pain, flooding every open space in his mind, a loosened tide of utter suffering: layered beneath the simple hurt of wounds (flashing razor's slash, infinite thorn-pricks) there wells a hollow-hearted despair thick as oil.

The doctor shudders and thrashes, trying to throw the child from his back as a dog shakes water. The tide of pain only rises. Barely aware of his own body under the drowning, he twists and forces the hand holding the hook to scrape along his own back until it catches on something not himself. Then with the strength of a dying animal he pulls the hook hard across, tearing the child off his back.

It still hangs on to his hand, scrambling to bite at his arm, but the doctor, freed from the blindness of pain, brings his booted foot down heavy on the child's chest, holding it and wrenching his hand free. As the child writhes under his boot, it turns onto its belly, and the doctor sees on its neck the loop of silver he knew would be there. He grabs the child's gritty hair with one hand and with the other swings down hard with the hook against that shining loop.

The hook clicks closed around the loop.

And, so hooked, the child's twisting body jerks and stiffens and goes suddenly motionless.

The doctor takes in a long, slow breath of camphor and diseased air. Somewhere farther away the wind is still howling against the darkness.

He lifts his boot from the child's back. It is still for another moment, then rises.

The doctor walks around it, inspecting. It looks nearly the same as it had before, except now it stands straight as a toy soldier. And its eyes, lid to lid, are now the same fresh white as its skin, only the red rims bright in contrast.

The doctor smooths the child's wild hair and nods, satisfied. He strides down the alley, scoops up his device, hefts his bag again into his gloved hand and walks back out to the street.

The child follows.

∽

By now the Madame has torn a page from her perfect ledger and is drawing on it.

The eyes of her paintings have mostly closed, asleep. But she can find no such soft oblivion. She is carefully pulling ink into patterns. Mountains. Rivers. A land far beyond her known world.

Her raven hops closer, its hard claws clicking against her desk, and cocks its head at her.

She continues drawing, waiting.

∼

Through the city streets the doctor and the child move, the doctor's robes billowing with every smooth stride. The child is his small white shadow.

So they flow on the inevitable rolling wave of time past a hundred darkened doors, a hundred shuttered windows. They pass stagnant pools full of twisting weeds, beggars indistinguishable from demons, alleys alight with glowing eyes.

The doctor considers his time here, quantifies and calculates it within the perfect ledger of his mind. He satisfies himself with the balance of his deeds.

This is his one life, long as it is. He must take his own path, sure as one step follows the next. This is his one life.

The child wades behind him through a foul puddle nearly up to its waist, unflinching.

∼

The eyes of the Madame's paintings open wide, then narrow. She ignores them and folds her drawing tidily in half and half again. She allows it a moment to sit neatly upon her desk before snatching it back up and crumbling it tight in her fist. When she opens her slim white fingers a clump of ashes is all that remains in her palm. And that only lingers for a second before it flutters apart, scattering gently across her desk like petals.

The raven glares at her, disapproving, but she shoos it off and it flies screaming up to the high mantle above the door. From behind the door come the heavy repetitive thuds of boots climbing up to her room. The stairs groan with each footfall. The Madame straightens her vest and, like her paintings, never takes her kohl-lined eyes from the door.

When the footfalls reach the top of the stairs, they stop. For a moment it is silent and only a thin panel of wood stands between her and the future.

Then the doorknob creaks and her raven hops back and forth, flapping its wings in a panic and the door bursts open slamming against the far wall. The paintings swing in their frames, eyes wild with helplessness.

The plague doctor stands in the doorway, long black coat and wide-brimmed hat blotting out the world beyond. His mask is smeared with filth. The medicine bag he carries is overstuffed and rimmed with stains. He is a creature of rot and despair. Regardless, a tide of passion rises in the Madame's bosom: a twisting riptide of joy and melancholy. And unbidden she feels a smirk appear on her lips. Delight in her own misery.

"It is time." The doctor's voice is barely audible, muffled behind his mask. Yet it seems to shake the floorboards.

"I know."

The doctor stands motionless.

The Madame can feel the air moving in and out of her body. Such mortal flesh.

"I have to go." His voice is heavy as an executioner's. "I cannot stay."

"I know. I don't want you to stay."

The doctor tilts his head, like the raven does, surprised.

She holds the words in her throat for a moment before releasing them. "I am going with you."

The sentiment is simple, but the doctor cocks his head even further, confused.

"I want to go with you," she says, tasting the sentence pass her lips as if it is a vile thing. Knowing even before he straightens himself, even before he speaks, that she will not get what she wants. And what if she did anyway? What was it worth, to abandon everything she had created for someone who would have left her? What was it worth, then, her own desire?

The doctor straightens himself. "No. I can bring nothing with me when I go."

She gives a curt nod, fury rising in her heart, a familiar pulse of blood and fire. "Your choice, I suppose." She gestures and the raven flutters back to her, perching now on her shoulder, glaring its beady eyes at the doctor. "You have come only to say goodbye?"

The mask sways side to side. "There are consequences to pleasure," the doctor says, stepping aside, revealing a small, pale child who takes three mechanical steps past the doctor and into the center of the room.

"What is that?"

"Our child."

She knows, already knows, but cannot believe it. The last time she saw it, it had been a tiny thing, fit to the palm of her hand. They had been together and it had appeared, as these things sometimes do to beings such as themselves — spontaneously from the vital heat of the air. She had lifted it by the silver loop on the back of its neck and it had gone limp as a kitten held by the scruff and she had laughed and they had tossed it out the window. She looks at the mechanical thing now and shakes her head. "Why bring it back?"

"It must be dealt with." Beneath his robe and mask she cannot tell how much he is mocking her. "We both must face it."

She sneers but feels her heart shuddering beneath her vest. "Take it with you."

He places his hand on the child's neck, on the glittering hook there. "I can bring nothing with me. Not even regrets."

Furious now, she pushes herself to her feet. "You wouldn't." But she can already see his thick gloved fingers curling around the metal.

He pulls out the hook and steps back. "Goodbye."

The child transforms, eyes suddenly pure red, little bony body crouching low as an animal ready to pounce. Growl down deep in its throat.

And all the boiling rage in the Madame's heart turns, in an instant, to ice cold fear.

∼

Even from the bottom stair, even from the street below, even from down the next alley, the doctor can hear the raven screaming and screaming and screaming.

The plague doctor walks in even strides now, paced perfectly as the heartbeat of a clock, long legs taking him swiftly through the spiderweb streets.

Spiked little corpse-eaters occasionally snarl up at him but otherwise he passes through the world like a shadow. An innocent being.

## ON THE OCCASION OF A BLOODLETTING

A perfect path unravels in his mind, a new future with twisted trees and mountain paths, a glorious future made right by following the only rules of his life worth remembering. The two rules of perfect freedom.
 Bring nothing with you.
 Leave nothing behind.

# ANY KIND OF FRIEND

## JACK KLAUSNER

AFTERWARDS — after the alley behind the bar and after I'm inside him, closing my eyes, letting myself go — I'll wonder whether he's done this before. I'll wonder whether I'm his first.

When he finds me, when he drifts over and climbs up on to the barstool next to mine, I'm sweat-damp and red-faced, five or six drinks in, trying to sit very still. They've got the heating on high and all the windows closed, so even though it's November it's suffocatingly hot, air so thick you could drink it.

Hey, he says with a voice like strings that might snap.

Slowly, I turn my head sideways.

He's skinny, colourless-seeming. Shaved head and sunken eyes, a black leather jacket that's in the process of swallowing him. He smells of cigarettes the way Dad used to.

Hi, I croak.

He puts an elbow on the bar and twists his body so he's facing more at me. He smiles. His face is so thin it's like the corners of his mouth maybe find their way around the sides, might hook around the hinges of his jaw. I wonder, briefly, whether he's a junkie. Or perhaps he's ill.

Michael, he says.

It takes me a moment to realise it's his name. It's not just the drink making me slow — I'm not used to this tennis game of talking. Out of practice. No friends, family all gone apart from Lianne who calls at Christmas, us managing two minutes on the phone before we run out of things.

But this guy, he sticks out his hand, and I'm getting a little quicker now, so I take it. We shake. I'm conscious of my sweaty palms, the way my face must shine in the bar light, the way my t-shirt's too tight around the soft body that grew around the one I used to have, a gradual smothering. This guy, he says it's good to meet me. Then he lets go of my hand and turns his attention to the TV mounted on the wall behind the bar. I follow his gaze and watch the warzone play out silently on the screen, the yellow subtitles coming up in blocks, occasional typos. Someone puts Def Leppard on the jukebox.

After a while, my glass is empty and the barman drifts my way. I open my mouth to say same again but the guy, Michael, he raises a hand, cuts across, says to the barman get two whiskies. A whisky each for me and my friend, is exactly what he says. I'll always remember that, I think. Someone calling me their friend.

We sit quietly, eyes on the TV. We sip our drinks. Def Leppard gives way to Scorpions. At some point, Michael swivels his stool so he's properly facing me, and now he's asking about my job — what do I do, where do I live, where am I from. And somehow I'm talking back, talking properly, telling him. People think if you're lonely and don't speak much, and then you have the chance, that it'll come out like diarrhea, but that's not how it is. Instead the words coming out my mouth feel funny, awkward, like misshapen things clambering out from between my teeth. But maybe it's the alcohol, too. Maybe I need to slow down.

Sandwich packing, I tell him. Nights.

Michael says how he lives on his own in a flat three blocks away. He works nights too but at a supermarket, keeps to himself, mostly. I ask about family and he says he's an only child, parents died in a crash when he was eighteen.

I've got an empty life, he says.

Sad, lonely little life, I say into my whisky glass as I tip it up and drink what's left.

He looks at me when I say that. Realising how it sounds, I tell him I only mean I know how he feels, because my life's the same.

When did it get like that? he asks.

I don't know. It just crept up.

Michael plays around with his glass, touches his fingertips all around the rim. He asks if I come here often. I tell him twice a week maybe, but I still don't know anyone — I've always been awkward.

And now Michael starts talking about how he thinks people either fit together or they don't, like jigsaw pieces. Not just romantically speaking, but in friendships, too. Like people fit certain people, or most people even, but some don't, some only fit a particular type of other people, maybe only one person out of everyone else. He says how a good friendship is something you carry around, inside, forever. Real friendships nourish, he says, real friends never let you down. The last whisky was the line, as I think of it, the threshold between on-the-way and drunk, so I'm nodding to all of this because it makes sense, all of it.

Michael talks and talks.

To *me*.

And I bathe in it.

And now somehow it's closing time and we're the last two in the bar, and the barman comes over and gently he says come on guys. I'm downing my whisky — when did Michael buy me another? — and I'm following Michael as he slips off his stool and stands there, swaying, until he heads towards the door, the barman saying goodnight guys, Michael raising a hand and saying goodnight back to him. And just like that I'm twisting around, looking over my shoulder, saying *night, man* like it's the most natural thing in the world.

Step outside, the cold hits like a bus. Michael slings an arm across my shoulders and leans his drunken weight on me. I look sideways at him and he's staring right back with his moon crater eyes and his wide smile, all these little teeth. When he breathes, what I get in my face is the sour smell of alcohol, bruised undertone of cigarette breath, and I think again of Dad.

I ask Michael if he'll be back tomorrow night, and he says his shifts are fucked so maybe, maybe not. What about swapping numbers, I ask — maybe we could meet up sometime. But he only raises an eyebrow and already I'm panicking because I'm messing this up.

We could be friends, I explain, hating the way my voice has gone all whiny.

We already are friends, he says back, standing in front of me now, grinning, clapping a hand down on my shoulder.

## ANY KIND OF FRIEND

I smile at the pavement. At the toes of my boots nearly touching the toes of his.

*Right?* he says.

Right, I'm saying back, and now I'm confessing: you're my first friend, Michael. My only friend.

All you need is one good one, he says.

Let me show you something, he says, and now he's grabbing my shoulder and dragging me towards the alley that runs up the side of the bar. It's darker in here. Colder, too. The smell of split bin bags and urine. Michael's this shape in front of me, eyes catching the streetlight glow — what little of it finds its way in here — and there's a glassiness to them, a wobble in his voice, and I realise he's crying. Let me show you, he keeps saying. And now there's a sound, unzipping, low and deep, and he's pulling his leather jacket apart like the petals of a great black flower. He's not wearing a top underneath, it's just bare skin, only that's not right, it's *not* just bare skin. Because there's an opening. A slit. A mouth, running vertically, one corner at the well of his throat, the other just above the dark shadow of the pubic hair breaching the waistband of his jeans. The mouth opens, closes. Flexing lips. It opens again, a little, and it's like he's breathing all over me again, sour drink and cigarette throat smell. I need you, he's saying. I'm starving, nourish me, if you were any kind of friend you would, if you were a real friend —

Frills emerge from between the lips like a hundred tongues. They glisten. They shiver.

The orifice opens again, the soft wet walls of his insides catching the weak light.

Come here, Michael's saying, voice thick and wet with phlegm, breath hitching in his throat. Please, come here, if you were any kind of friend —

I take a step towards him.

That's right, he says as I reach out, as I brush the wet frills with the tips of my fingers.

I knew I could count on you, he whispers, body trembling as I slowly part the lips.

You'll never be lonely again, Michael sighs.

And now he gasps. Moans.

As I lean forward.

As I climb in.

# ASTER

## ELIN OLAUSSON

THE SEED CAME from one of the women travelers heading for the temple at the end of the road. It was big and lumpy, the size of a beetle, and Linna didn't want to accept it at first. She tried to ignore the woman's outstretched hand, but the woman wouldn't have it.

"You've given me tea and bread, though I can tell that you have barely enough for yourself. This is your reward. Plant it in the shade, give it water and time. It will be of use to you."

The woman's bare feet were ashen from the road, and the marks on her hands spoke of sacred rites in moonlight. Linna didn't want to ask. She fed travelers if they asked, since that was how she had been raised, but she had no need for their talk and godliness. After the woman had left she clutched the seed in her hand, not sure what to think of it. The temple-seekers were a strange sort, no one knew quite what they were up to in their sacred halls. Perhaps she should have declined the offer, but it was too late now and the seed was hers. After a few minutes of pondering she went up to the patch of dirt beneath the blackcurrant bushes and dug a hole, dropped the seed in it. There. She went back inside, to churn butter and knead dough and sweep dusty floors, and soon she had forgotten all about the woman's promise.

It started sprouting two weeks later. A single stalk, thin as a cat's whisker, pale as milk. She was on her knees picking berries when she saw it, and it was a full minute before she realized what it was. It looked strange, fungal, like it could cause sickness and possibly death. Linna didn't want it near her blackcurrants, but she recalled the woman's words and besides, it was the first gift she had received in a long time. Maybe, if she was just patient like her parents had taught her, the milk-white stalk would grow into something pretty.

A month later, the head started to show. Of course, she didn't know it was a head at first, not until the ears popped up like baby chanterelles next to the big, egg-like shape in the middle. Only then did she realize that the stalks were hair and that they had darkened since she spotted the first one. They weren't milky now but a soft, citrusy shade of yellow, and she didn't like them anymore than she had at first. And when she closed her eyes at night she thought about the fact that all heads have noses, eyes, and teeth-filled mouths, and the strange thing growing beneath her blackcurrant bushes must have them, too.

It was another week before the neck emerged. By then she knew that the face, however it looked, was turned the other way, and all she could see was the back of a head sparsely covered with hair. It was rumpled, some strands hanging down while others pointed straight up, and she toyed with the idea of slipping a comb into her apron pocket before she went into the garden in the morning. But the thought of touching the thing revolted her, as if the whisker-hair would come to life and seize her. As if touching it would be some sort of invitation.

Shoulders, back, and arms, all sinewy and pale like a malnourished weed. It bothered her that the thing was naked, but then again, it made sense that it was. At night she sat in the nook by the front door, window open, the garden humming, blossoming, living. If she squinted, she could see the thing, but only barely. From a distance it might as well have been a rock, and she didn't know whether or not she would have preferred it to be.

The process was fast after the hands emerged, as if he had pushed himself out of the ground. When she'd started to think of him as *he* she didn't know; it had happened gradually, but perhaps the sight of his fingers was the turning point. They were long and limp, but still undoubtedly human. Every once in a while they twitched, a movement that made her think of the earthworms she'd picked up from the road as a child, and how they had squirmed in her outstretched palm.

It was only three days later that he bloomed. Linna knew that it was happening, knew from the sight of his big feet, half-covered in dirt. Still, she yelped when he stepped out of the garden patch, with a snapping noise, and turned to face her.

His face had a strange sheen to it and would have been nice to look at if it weren't for the eyes, pinprick small and dirty-looking, as if they'd been smudged with a layer of dust. Pointy nose, large mouth, lips like the slugs that ate her leek and lettuce. There were other things to notice, too, things her mother would have frowned at, so she dashed inside and came back with the baby blanket that had just been lying in the linen cupboard ever since her own distant childhood. He didn't understand what to do with it so she wrapped it around his hips, tucked the ends in neatly. Being so close, she smelled the earth on him, like the garden after a summer rain. It wasn't an unpleasant scent but it wasn't what a man was supposed to smell like, so she turned her face away.

"Can you talk?"

No, of course he could not. He didn't even try, just stood there with hanging arms, the woolen blanket straining around his thighs. But when Linna retreated to the house he followed, a gangly form, a human-shaped thing that wasn't human. She made him sit at the table, gave him a glass of fresh well water. It amused her to see him lift it to his wide mouth and have a sip — this, then, was knowledge he was born with.

"Glass. Mouth. Water." She pointed, nodded, repeating the words. "Linna," she said, placing her hand on her chest, and he watched her with those pinprick eyes, saying nothing.

She named him Aster because he had sprouted from the soil, because he was autumnal and tall. He deserved a floral name but not a beautiful one, nothing to do with roses. After an hour of searching she found her father's old shirt and trousers, the clothes he had died in, but Aster hadn't objected to the blanket and would hardly care about wearing a dead man's clothing. The shirt was a little small but it wasn't as if her own garments didn't have holes and tears in them. He had a limp, she noticed, one foot dragging a little behind the other. It didn't seem to bother him, so she didn't bring it up. It annoyed her, though, that irregularity, just like she was annoyed by his silence and his tiny eyes. Maybe an animal had attacked his foot while he was still growing, or he had injured it when he broke free from the ground. The images kept her awake that night: bite-marks on his pale skin, pieces of skin and bone sticking out of the garden patch beneath her blackcurrant bushes. But when she went to check in the morning there was nothing there, and his feet had no marks on them.

She gave him tasks, because she didn't know what else to do with him. He was terrible in the kitchen — broke saucers, splashed dishwater everywhere — but excelled at gardening. She handed him a shovel, told him where to dig, and an hour later she had a new flower patch beneath the bedroom window.

"Seeds. Here." She watched as he dropped each seed into the ground, carefully covering them with soil. When he was done his hands were filthy, and she brought him inside to scrub his nails, that were thin and sharp like a tiny child's.

"I can't remember what flowers will come from those seeds," she said. Her mother had left heaps of brown paper envelopes, some neatly labelled, but not all. "We'll have to wait and see."

Aster had slept on the floor the first night, stretched out under the baby blanket that didn't cover more than his upper body. He hadn't complained, but she didn't like the thought of him there, a big white lump staining her floor.

"Sleep here," she said that night, lifting her bedcovers. "It's more comfortable."

His body filled the space, pushed her close to the edge of the bed. The first man she had shared a bed with, but she wasn't sure he was a man at all. He made no sound, no movements, and in the morning he woke when she did. The soft light of dawn fell on his back, made it look boneless. Tissue and fat, whipped-cream skin, but no bone.

Aster ate little and didn't seem curious about the food on her plate, as if it couldn't possibly concern him. He drank water after working, but frowned at her teas and the half-empty bottle of cider. Linna found that he was more agreeable to her when he had his back turned. She found that she couldn't see his pinprick eyes at night, or his foot, or the sickly hue of his skin. One night she removed her shift before going to bed, and her nudity seemed to be the signal he needed. He was strong, heavy, and if she breathed through her mouth she couldn't smell the earth on him. After that first time it became a pattern, a task to complete like stoking the fire or washing in the morning. She didn't exactly want him there, but he was. She might as well take what he offered.

Once every month she had to walk to town to get her flour, her sugar, her salt and spices. It took half a day to get there and half a day to get back, and she told Aster the night before to make sure he understood.

"You will have to stay inside until I come back. You mustn't get anywhere near the fire. You mustn't break anything. If you're good, I might bring back a gift for you."

When she left the cottage at dawn he stood in the doorway, watching her with those ugly eyes. She tried to comb his hair every morning but it was a mess no matter what she did, and for a moment the sight of those sparse, yellowish strands made her nauseous.

She was at the gate when she heard it:

"Inna."

Instantly, she knew what the sound was and where it had come from. But she opened the gate and walked — walked fast, before he could say her name again.

She returned in the evening, feet sore, joints aching from the bag slung over her back. It had occurred to her in town that she should have brought Aster along, made him carry the groceries, but the thought of being seen with him in public was mortifying. He sat hunched over the table when she entered the cottage, face blank, arms resting against his thighs. The sight enraged her, and she didn't know why.

"You're so useless you can't even cook." She put the flour and sugar in the pantry, shoved the marmalade jars aside. "I've been walking all day. I'm tired."

He didn't say anything. Of course he didn't. But once they were in bed he turned to her, sniffling, wheezing.

"Inna. Inna."

His worm-fingered hands on her skin, pawing, and she knew that it had to happen. Tonight, but tonight only.

Killing him was the simplest thing. The next morning she told him to dig up the garden patch beneath the blackcurrant bushes, dig deep into the soil, and he did it just as he did everything she asked. There were two shovels, not just the one, and when the hole was wide enough she struck him over his pale, ugly head. It took three strikes, four, five, but after that he fell into a heap of boneless flesh, and all she had to do was push him into the hole. His pinprick eyes were open and his mouth, too, so she filled up the hole with dirt until they were gone.

*Inna.*

After having a bath, she looked from the window into the garden and saw that it was empty, as it should. Her house was all hers again, and her garden, too. She ate her lonely supper that night, went to bed with her shift on.

It wasn't as if he had been human. His hanging arms, that foot he had dragged along. The eyes that had followed her. It was better this way, she told herself. It was how it should be.

Still, she hoped that the traveling woman would return someday and bring a different seed, one without flaws, one that deserved the name of a rose. But the woman never came.

# ECDYSIS

## JESS KOCH

AT NIGHT, I hear it in the walls. Something moving through the insulation, the wiring, the empty spaces between the studs. At night, my mind tumbles over all the things it might be. I listen for some clue: a breath, a whine, the chittering of rodents. Mice, squirrels, chipmunks. None are out of the question. I think about when I was six and my brother told me about rat kings. At that age, I could only picture the character from some cartoon version of *The Nutcracker* but now I picture a swirling mound of rats, some half-dead, some already dead, moving through the walls and all knotted up by their tails, dragged along by those still alive. At night, I stay in my daughter's room and hold her close. Her small body still fits comfortably in my arms, against my chest.

It knows where we sleep, like it's circling prey, waiting. So I don't sleep. I listen all night as it moves from one wall to another, sometimes going quiet for hours only to resurface in the wall behind the bed.

I call an exterminator even though I can't afford it. When he arrives at the house, he asks me if I live alone. He asks me where my husband is. Dead, I tell him, even though it isn't true. Might not be true. I guess it could be, but he was never my husband. The exterminator wears a green uniform with a cheerful racoon patch over his heart. He brings in strange equipment from his car and walks slowly through all the rooms in the house, tapping on the walls, listening. I hear it worst in the bedroom, I tell him. He goes in the attic and the basement and the outside of the house. In the end, he hands me a bill for too much money and tells me there is nothing living in my walls and there's no evidence anything ever was. He says, you're probably just hearing your neighbors in the next townhouse over — shared walls and all that.

I will have to cancel my daughter's next dentist appointment to pay for the exterminator. That night, I watch her brush her teeth with a Disney pink toothbrush and can't get the thought out of my head of all her teeth turning black and popping out of her gums, scattering like corroded pearls all over the bathroom floor.

∿

I move us to the living room and try to make a game out of it. I tell my daughter we're building a fort to sleep in for a few nights. It's fun, I tell her, I used to do this when I was your age. I don't know if she hears the thing in the walls, but I don't ask because I need to pretend she doesn't.

We set up chairs from the kitchen in the middle of the room and drape blankets over them. We bring in every pillow and strip our beds of quilts and sheets and arrange them on the floor between the chairs. I drag the old television I've had since childhood to the edge of the fort. Its cords run taut across the floor. The television is hooked up to a satellite dish that only sometimes works and definitely not when it's raining but I find an old sitcom through the static and we curl up on the pillows. In here, the rest of the house doesn't exist. Nothing lives in these blanket walls. I listen to the studio audience laugh at jokes that aren't funny anymore and wonder how many of them are dead now. My daughter's breath is warm on my wrist where I hold her tucked to my body. Before she was born, my body was her house, my skin her walls. She was safe then. Another episode of the same show begins, and I think I should open my eyes and catch the intro so I can see what it's called but I can't and soon after that, I'm asleep.

∿

I wake to the gray static of a dead channel filling the fort in colorless light. It's colder now and I reach out into the tangle of pillows and blankets for my daughter's warmth, to bring her close again. But my hands do not find her. I sit up and throw all the blankets off and see that her side of our makeshift bed is empty. I try not to let the panic seep in; she has just started using the bathroom on her own without waking me. That's probably where she's gone.

I stumble out of the fort and trip over the television cords, ripping them from the wall and snuffing out its light and static hush. The room feels strange in this darkness. I turn on the hall light, but it seems too dim, like a fog has settled in the house.

The bathroom door is open, the room empty. So is her bedroom, so is mine. I check the closets where she used to hide when she was scared. I call out for her. I run from room to room, lighting the house up with every bulb that hasn't burned out. I think about checking outside. I think about calling the police or waking the neighbors but then I hear it. Louder now than before as though it has grown. The house creaks as it moves, working its way down the hall toward the bedrooms.

I find a hammer in the toolkit in the coat closet — the one my brother bought me when I first moved into this house, just me and her. You have to learn to fix the dumb shit, he told me. You can't afford to pay someone for every little thing.

I think about this as I drive the hammer into the drywall. A photo falls face down from its home, and I hear the glass crack. It's a photo of me in the hospital right after she was born. My eyes are red, my forehead a glaze of sweat. I remember her so clearly then, a perfect lump of squishy skin in my arms, wailing with the force of brand-new lungs. Face red with fresh blood.

My mother used to tell me I would be a bad mom. With your issues, she used to say. A part of me wonders if I had my daughter in some way to prove her wrong but I think it probably just proves her right. What kind of person has a child just to spite their mother who was dead before she was born?

The wall is soft and a hole begins to form like a gaping toothless mouth. I reach inside and feel the thing slide against my fingers, moving through the wall. It's a texture I can't explain; both smooth and rough at once, slightly cool to the touch, like snakeskin.

It reminds me of when I was a kid living near the mountains in

**ECDYSIS**

Tennessee and my next-door neighbor had a ball python named Lilith. I still remember the way it felt as she wound around my wrist, trying to decide if my arm was a threat worth constricting to death. One day, the snake escaped her enclosure and for months, we kept thinking we were going to find her with one of our hens halfway down her throat. We never did see Lilith again, but I still dream about her almost every night.

I flinch and pull my hand back as the giant thing works its way past the hole in the wall and vanishes into the bowels of the house. With the hammer and my hands, I tear away the wall until there is a hole large enough for me to fit through. I get a flashlight and crawl into the dark, squeezing my body sideways and inching through the inside of the wall. It's so tight, I can't fill my lungs.

A few feet in, I hit a beam I can't get past. I shine the light and see nothing but wires and dust and more studs. Then I cast it upward and I am staring into my own face, hanging down from above. A serpent's tongue flicks from between its lips. Beyond the neck, a long snake body of shimmering black is coiled around the studs.

∼

I call the cops and tell them my daughter is missing. I don't tell them about the snake-thing in the walls, they won't believe me.

The man on the phone asks if she's a runaway. No, she's barely four. What about her dad? Out of the picture. How out of the picture? I don't know, at least a few states and a drug addiction out of the picture. We need his info anyway, he says, then after a long pause asks me if I'm sure that my daughter isn't just staying with friends or relatives. Maybe you forgot, he says, it happens more often than you'd think.

I tell him I want a search party. He asks me if I have a recent photo of her, but I don't and a sour feeling stews in my stomach. I don't have a camera, I tell him, but this is a lie. There's a Polaroid camera in the cupboard above the fridge with a brand-new pack of film still in its box. I ask him to send them to my house first, she may have gotten lost in the walls.

No one comes. The phone rings and it's a different officer this time. She sounds too young to be a cop. She asks me if I'm still taking my medications. She means the ones on the bathroom sink. I ask her why they haven't come to search the house. Ma'am we have searched your house, maybe you just don't remember.

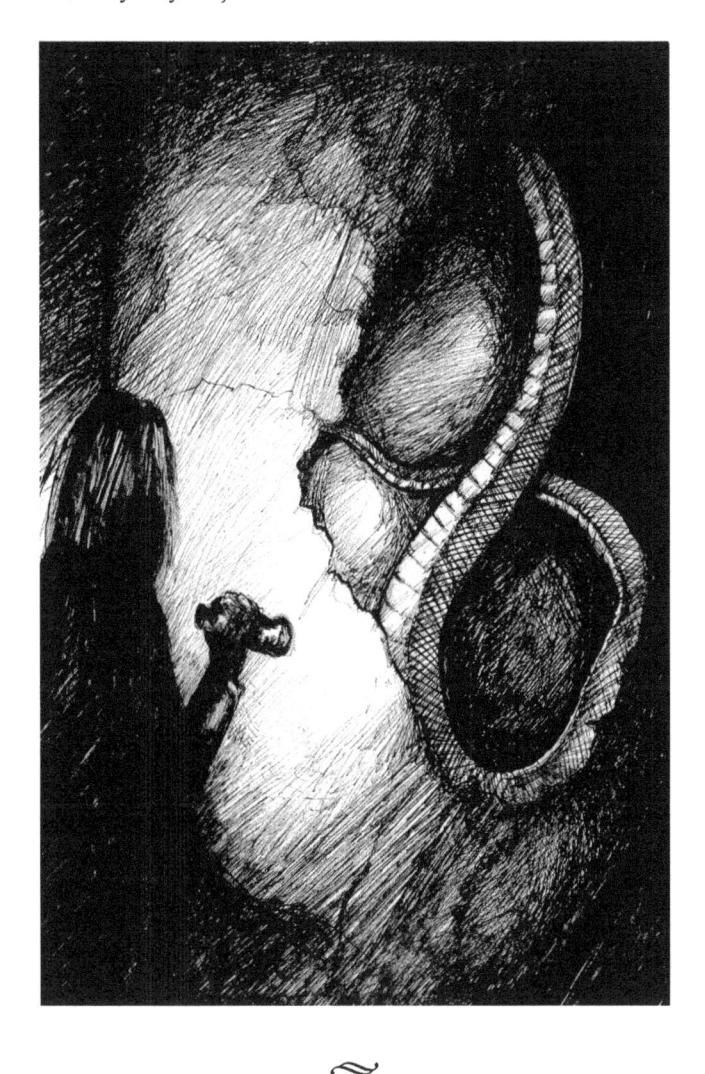

∽

I press my ear to every wall but hear nothing. I wait for the phone to ring again but it doesn't. In the shed out back, I find a sledgehammer from when my brother helped me demolish the old bathroom. I know she's still in the house; I can feel the tether between us — where I imagine an umbilical cord used to be.

I start in her bedroom. The walls take a few hits before they start to collapse. Billows of white dust cloud the room, coat my lungs, sting my eyes but still I swing at her Care Bear posters and her yellow shelf of cardboard books I hung last month.

The holes take shape. There is only empty space behind her walls. I move down the hall and expand the existing hole there. I do the other wall too. And the living room, the kitchen, the bathroom. Knocking holes, peering inside, seeing nothing but shadows staring back at me.

My bedroom is last, but that's where, in the wall behind my bed, I find the egg. Pillow-sized and off-white and so smooth to the touch the surface almost feels like water.

I wonder, briefly, if I should call the cops again. But no, I don't want them to take it from me. The egg is heavy and warm and I'm barely able to carry it to the bathroom. I place it into the tub on a nest of damp towels and then swaddle it in blankets from the dismantled fort. The only thing I know about eggs is that you're supposed to keep them warm.

∼

I should take my pills, but lately, they've made me feel like I'm dreaming while I'm awake. At the supermarket a few weeks back, I left without my daughter. I drove all the way home, unpacked the groceries, and laid down for a nap before I realized she was not at home with me. The worst part of all of it was that I'd forgotten I had a daughter at all.

The phone rings in the evening. It's my brother. I see his number appear on the caller ID screen, but I don't answer. He doesn't leave a message. He never does.

I fall asleep in my daughter's bed in her room of crumbling drywall and a white film coating every surface, even the bare mattress. My arms are sore from swinging and my head feels heavy.

I wake in the dark because I hear it moving and I rush to the bathroom, watching from the doorway as it slithers through an opening in the wall and coils itself around the egg. The thing rests its face — my face — on the edge of the porcelain tub. Eyes like yellow cat-eye marbles.

∼

The next morning, someone knocks on my door. It's the man from next door. He and his wife moved in a few months back. Before that, their townhouse was empty; I preferred it that way. He's wearing a white bathrobe and has three bound up newspapers tucked under his arm. I heard a lot of banging coming from over here, he says. His tongue sprays spittle as he talks. Then he says, my wife just had a baby, and everyone needs their sleep, so. He scratches the stubble on his jawline and it makes me dislike him even more. I don't know what you're talking about, I tell him, I didn't hear anything.

I watch him walk back down my front steps and up his own, only a few feet away. His wife is waiting for him on their porch, and she tosses her hands in the air in response to his shrug.

Something about the way the man walks reminds me of *him*. I met my daughter's dad at a gas station in Ohio. It's not a romantic story. It's not a story worth telling. He knows he has a daughter but has never met her. He moves around a lot, gets evicted a lot. Not that any of it matters except to say the cops probably won't find him and even if they do, he won't have her. He never wanted her. Not like I did.

∽

Later that night, in the hallway outside the bathroom, I find a snakeskin. A hollowed-out white casing of diamond-patterned skin. The shedding is as long as the hall and leads to my daughter's room.

The egg is no longer in the bathroom, but the delicate remains of its shell litter the bottom of the tub, suspended in a viscous fluid mixed with what might be blood.

I step lightly over the snakeskin, down the hall, to the open door of her bedroom. And she is there, on the bed, a red-faced infant once again with that soft, squishy skin. She is resting in cradled arms, both of them naked and wet and asleep. The thing that is not me looks just as I do now, her scales and snake body gone, replaced by skin and limbs that hold my daughter too close.

I back away, sinking, sinking toward the wall across from her bed. The other me opens her eyes and they are just like mine now, too. She watches me as she kisses my daughter on the top of her head, pulls her even closer. I can still feel that wisp of hair against my mouth, the smell of her baby skin. I want her in my arms but I'm too tired and I

## ECDYSIS

let my back slide down the broken wall, let my eyes succumb to the heavy sway of sleep.

∼

When I wake, they're gone. The bed has a subtle impression where their bodies used to be. I think they must have gone back into the walls, so I take the sledgehammer to all the ones that are still intact, opening the house up like a cadaver to be gutted.

In one heavy swing to the living room, the head of the sledgehammer breaks through the other side of the wall. Dim violet light spills out from the hole and I lean in. It's a small room with bunny wallpaper, a cloud-shaped rug, and a nightlight glowing from the corner beneath a circular window. Just below the hole I've made, she is there. Pink-skinned and fast asleep in a crib. Her tiny chest fluttering with breath, with a heart beating.

The hole is just large enough to reach through, to gently lift her from her bed. She's lighter than I thought she would be — lighter than I remember. I pull her with careful arms through the hole and bring her warmth to my chest. It's okay, I whisper, you're with me now. Despite my calming words, she wakes and begins to cry. I bounce her in my arms like I used to and bring her to the remains of the blanket fort. I place her down on the pillows and rebuild the fort around her.

She smells just like I remember. I kiss her feather-soft hair. I wonder where the other me has gone; maybe she won't come back. I watch as my daughter settles back into an easy sleep. I put a hand on her chest and feel it rise and fall beneath my palm. I'll never sleep again.

Later, there are sounds outside. The search party I was promised. But I don't need their help anymore. They are calling for someone, for my daughter, but I can't make out their words. I wonder if my neighbor is out there in his bathrobe, yelling with his wet mouth through a rolled-up newspaper.

I take my daughter down the hallway and slip into the space between the walls, where we won't be found. I hear it again, the house creaking as something moves through its walls. But I am the thing in the walls, now. My skin itches, like a fire is smoldering in my bones. With my fingernails, I scratch at my arm, deep enough to draw blood. Drops of red slip down my skin, staining her pajama onesie. It's only then I notice the bunnies on the fabric — the same ones from the wallpaper in the room through the wall. A layer of sticky flesh peels away from my arm and underneath is a shimmer of black scales.

Someone knocks on the door, but I push further and further into the dark, until the space is so tight, I can't breathe. The phone rings and I hear them out there in the streets, on my steps, inside the townhouse next to mine, and I'm sure of it now — yes — they're calling my name.

# RIGOR

## ALISON MOORE

WHEN THE FIRST person went missing, locals suspected the bog. Even children, *especially* children, knew not to go there, but the missing person was from out of town and was said to be a walker.

"Why anyone would want to go walking in that desolate place, I don't know," said Floyd's dad. He was deep in the cupboard under the stairs, sweeping up the last of the glass, working his brush into the corners.

"Perhaps he was exploring," said Floyd, who had finished his coffee and was looking around for somewhere to put the empty cup.

His dad, emerging from the understairs cupboard to tip the contents of the dustpan into the bin, said, "But there's nothing there. There's nothing to see. Just the bloody bog." The sound of the glass shards sliding and hitting the bottom of the bin set Floyd's teeth on edge. His dad's home-brew, still fermenting in the bottles, had burst out and flooded, filthy, into the hallway, ruining the carpet and filling the house with a foul yeasty stench. "He's a damn fool."

Floyd looked across at his mother, who was standing at the window, staring out at the dark garden, and did not appear to be listening. Floyd got to his feet and said, to the back of her head, "I'd better be getting home."

"All right," she said, and after a moment she turned and followed him to the door, her scent of lilies wafting around her.

"You're not planning on indulging in that nonsense of yours, are you?" his dad called after him. "Bloody ridiculous, and you a scientist."

But there was no discrepancy, thought Floyd; his approach was rigorous. "I'll see you," he said to his mother, who did not like to be kissed, and who closed the door smartly after him.

Floyd's own home was larger and more attractive than his parents' house, in which he felt cramped and uncomfortable, but he could walk from one to the other in a matter of minutes. From his parents' front gate, he had only to cross the river and climb the hill. It was easier going up than going down, which was hard on the knees.

The cloud-covered moon hung high in the sky and he climbed through the drizzle towards it.

Where his parents' house was new and neat, with double glazing and a crew-cut lawn, his own was old and sprawling, the garden neglected and overgrown, but his front door was solid and the walls were thick, and he was glad of the space.

He closed his front door behind him, stamped the dirt from his boots, hung his coat on its peg. "All right," he said to the darkness in the hallway, "now we'll see."

He had everything he needed in the kitchen: a nip of brandy first of all, and then his Ouija board. He sat in candlelight, in his socks, asking his questions in the same voice he used on the phone: "Are you there? Can you hear me?" He sat there until his candle burnt low, until his brandy glass was empty, until his feet and fingers grew cold. There was nothing. *Damn fool.* He pushed away from the table, his chair legs scraping over the flagstones, and took himself to bed.

∼

"The usual?" said the landlord.

"The usual," said Floyd, "and a packet of peanuts." He took his pint to his regular corner, where Mikey was already waiting.

"Any joy?" asked Mikey.

"Not yet," said Floyd.

"Are you going to keep trying?"

"Oh yes," said Floyd, "I'll keep trying." He drank deeply from his pint. He told Mikey he'd been thinking that perhaps it took some time for the spirits to come out, the way an odour — the smell of dying flowers, the smell of a dead mouse — grew stronger, more pronounced, from one day to the next.

"It's a question of patience, then," said Mikey.

"And," said Floyd, through a mouthful of peanuts, "persistence."

∼

When the Marks boy went missing later that month, and stayed missing, the boy's mother came to Floyd's door to ask for his help. It was known that Floyd used a Ouija board, and the woman was desperate.

"I've already tried it," he told her. "I'm not getting anything."

She begged him, on her knees on his doorstep, to try again.

"I will," he said, "I'll keep trying," but he would not let her stay; he could not do it, he told her, with anyone else in the room.

Alone at his kitchen table, in near darkness, with his inch of brandy to warm him and his feet flat on the floor, he asked, "Are you there?" His voice went beseechingly into the dim and flickering corners and there was a miserable lack of response.

He had to tell the Marks woman, when she came again, that he had not been able to speak to her son, and she thought perhaps that meant there was hope but the whole thing put Floyd in a terrible mood. He didn't know what it meant, that he could not reach a spirit. The truth was, sitting there with his Ouija board, he had never once had a response. He had sometimes wondered if a Ouija board could be defective, if he had a dud, but he had tried more than one with no joy. And yet he knew that there *were* spirits; even as a child, he had known that.

He'd been about five, spending the night in a guest house somewhere on the Scottish coast with his parents. They had a family room, but when he woke in the night in a strange bed in the dark, and called for his mother, nobody came. Floyd did not know where he was, or what time it was, or where his mother had gone. He got out of bed and went barefoot to the door, which was closed but not locked. He opened it just enough to stand in the gap and look out at the dim landing, rubbing the Sandman's grit from his eyes and seeing the lady made of fog. That's what he called her, in the morning, at the breakfast table. "There was a lady made of fog," he said, "standing at the top of the stairs." "Is that right?" said his dad, glancing at Floyd's mother. Floyd, who knew that look, insisted she had been there, he had seen her. He felt, too, that she knew he was there, though she didn't turn towards him. He had watched her going through the wall. "Soft in the head," said his dad, when Floyd was out of the room. Out in the hallway, five-year-old Floyd was looking up at the landing, looking for the fog lady, but she wasn't there in the daytime, perhaps she was still in the wall, or at least she wasn't visible, and after lunch they went home.

From time to time, someone would mention the fog lady — not just his parents but uncles and aunts and family friends. "Here she comes," someone would say, as the steam rose from the kettle, and, "There she is," when smoke billowed from a car exhaust. They would not tell him where the guest house had been, "because," said his dad, "you'll go back there and embarrass yourself." Floyd insisted on what he had seen, but as he grew older he learnt to be more secretive, and pursued his interest in the spirit world behind closed doors.

Wearily, he left the table and his Ouija board, rinsed his brandy glass and blew his candle out.

∽

His dad, glancing up from the sports page, said, "Have you heard from your sister?"

"Not for a while," said Floyd. "I guess she's busy."

"You both keep yourselves to yourselves," said his dad. It was hard to tell if it was a complaint or advice.

"I guess I'll get going," said Floyd, finding the home-brew's lingering stink unbearable, glancing towards his mother as he got to his feet.

∽

"The usual?"

"The usual," said Floyd, "and a couple of packets of peanuts." He joined Mikey in their corner.

"No joy?" said Mikey.

"No," said Floyd. He'd been considering the reasons a spirit might remain, because surely not all spirits did. He said to Mikey, "Have you ever seen a ghost?"

"Never have," said Mikey.

"But you believe they exist?"

"Well," said Mikey, "*you've* seen one, haven't you?"

"Just that once," said Floyd. Unfinished business, he thought. Trauma, anger, a sense of injustice. And a connection with a particular place, or a particular person.

"You going to keep trying?" asked Mikey.

"Yes," said Floyd, "I'll keep trying."

"Not that I really know how it works."

"Come back to mine and see for yourself." Floyd drank what was left in his pint glass down in one go and got to his feet. "Get you another?" he said to Mikey, who would match Floyd pint for pint and chaser for chaser, despite his small stature, and even then Floyd had never once seen him anything other than softly spoken, mild mannered.

"Yeah," said Mikey. "Cheers, mate."

∽

"It's kind of spooky," said Mikey, crossing the threshold. "Where's the light switch?"

"We'll leave the lights off," said Floyd. "I've got candles."

"It's really spooky," said Mikey, peering up the stairs.

"But that's the problem," said Floyd. "It's really not. It's just old."

"And dark."

"It's three hundred years old," said Floyd, "but if any of its occupants died here, it doesn't seem as if they left a ghost." He sometimes roamed the house at night and was always disappointed.

"It's so big."

"It's too big for just me," said Floyd, looking up at the empty landing, beyond which were all the empty bedrooms and bathrooms and the silence of the attic.

"Have your parents been to visit yet?"

"Not yet," said Floyd. "My dad might come to cut the grass." His dad would find the state of the place unforgiveable. "I don't know if my mother will come."

"You've got a cellar," said Mikey, who had opened an understairs door.

"Yes," said Floyd.

## RIGOR

"What's that for?" asked Mikey. "Have you got, like, wine?"

"I'll take you down later," said Floyd, leading his friend down the hallway towards the kitchen.

~

He had to turn the lights on to clean the kitchen floor, though it spoilt the atmosphere. "You've never let me down yet, Mikey," he said as he scrubbed at the flagstones and the gaps in between.

It was probably too soon, but still he laid out the Ouija board and poured his measure of brandy. Or perhaps this was good, while the trauma was still fresh. He sat down and took a deep breath. "Are you there?" he said. "Can you hear me?" And then he waited, in the dancing light of a new candle, to see if this time he would have any joy.

# LONG SCISSORS, BLACK CANDLES

PERRY RUHLAND

THE BOYS HAD AGREED to gather in the far meadow at moonrise per Victor's instructions. The older boy had spoken to his followers at lunch, where, with his signature talent for the oblique and enticing, he alluded to making some fantastic discovery the night before, and said he would generously reveal its nature to all who brought a pair of long-bladed scissors and a tall, black candle — only black would suffice.

    The meadow was their usual haunt, a small patch of untamed land which lay at the crown of a rocky hill. The boys suspected that they were the only ones who knew of its existence, as the path up the hill was hidden by thorny brambles, and the meadow itself was nestled within a dense halo of shadowed woodland which, from a distance, appeared as a single impenetrable thicket. From the secret path, one could see the nearby town in miniature: a glowing mass of jails and churches that fanned out like the ripples of a whirlpool from the great columned schoolhouse. But once inside the curious meadow, that ordered world was gone; in the midst of the feral grasses and dim-glowing nightcaps, the suffocating miasma of adult society and the straight-jacket of their terribly adult laws were revealed as nothing more than juvenile abstractions, no more dangerous than the monsters the boys once believed lurked under their beds.

## LONG SCISSORS, BLACK CANDLES

That night the meadow was beset by a low tide of puffy fog. Max was the first to arrive, and he sat upon his favored throne of jagged rock whose peak rose scarcely above the mist. He made a big show of his position when Lyonel emerged from the path, although the gaunt boy, as usual, greeted his taunts with a stiff smile. Of course Lyonel was soon joined by Fritz, and the two sat together on the dewy grass. The pair shared a clove cigarette while Max began an unprompted rant about his younger brother, who evidently had once again stolen something or other from his room, and would have to be beaten the next day before it was retrieved. Karel, the youngest of the sect, arrived for the tail-end of the story, although he wasn't noticed until after it ended — the boy was small and skeletal, his presence generally confined to the distant corners of incurious eyes.

With all assembled, it was only a matter of time before conversation turned to Victor, or more specifically, to Victor's absence. It was not unusual for their leader to be late to his own meetings, although given his rather frantic character displayed that afternoon, Fritz found his tardiness a cause for concern. Max insisted it was only another trick — and a tired one, too — but even he had to admit that Victor seemed different. None of the boys could ever honestly say they were fully comfortable around their leader, but neither could they imagine him as having anything short of complete control over not only his actions but, on enchanted nights not unlike these, the universe. Still it was agreed that something was off that day, what Lyonel described as an unusual pallid tint to Victor's cheeks and a hint of some jittering anticipation behind his silver eyes.

While the others gossiped, Karel watched the night. Up in the meadow, the astronomical effects always seemed closer than they were at home, even still that night the waxing moon hung perilously low, its sharp edges glowing bone-white. Watching its cratered blade, Karel's mind wandered from the sky, past the shadowed woods, down the hidden path and back to the dozing village where he'd been an hour before, in the little house, eating a thin supper. The gazes had slipped past him again: the eyes of his mother, red and puffy, and those of his father, so small behind his heavy spectacles. Karel ate in silence while they talked about the price of the doctor and the care for the girl in the nursery; while they mourned the wan future that awaited the boy seated invisibly right across the table.

After dinner, mother went up to the nursery and father shuffled outside its splintering door; neither noticed Karel leave. For a long time now he felt neither cared. And as the moon dragged across the sky and the mist around the boys rose to veil the peaks of the darkened woods, that was all Karel thought of. In thinking, he felt nothing at all.

A shout roused him from his wallowing — it was Max, up on his rock, bony finger jutting at something in the gray expanse. Evidently, Victor had arrived. His silhouette rambled through the fog — tall and wiry, framed by a frayed coat and carrying a small basket. His gnarled cane, a favored and characteristically ostentatious affect, bobbed at his side. Before his features could even be discerned, Max yelled—

"Moonrise, freak, you said moonrise!"

—and the shadow only laughed.

Although they all spent countless hours in his presence, on certain occasions the sight of Victor's face still managed to startle his followers. Fritz couldn't help but twitch as the boy's death's-head emerged, a thin film of pale skin stretched tight across what seemed an irregularly angular skull. In the darkness of the glade, shadows mobbed the floors of his sunken eyes and engulfed his neck, creating the illusion that his head hovered slightly above his night-black attire. He grinned, sharp teeth flaring.

"What took you so long?" asked Max.

"This," Victor said, placing the covered basket between his seated followers, "has been rather difficult today."

The basket was familiar to all assembled. A self-styled Prometheus, Victor had stolen the flames of the adult world to share with his wretched people, enlightening them in the harsher, stranger reaches of life. From that basket Victor had given black wines that shimmered in the starry night, oblong pills which hatched strange and fitful dreams, and folios crammed with images of adults in bizarre and violent positions, bruised legs and malefic grins, performing vivid acts the boys couldn't explain — and which Victor refused to.

"What's inside?"

"Patience, Lyonel, patience. First — did everyone bring what was requested? Yes? Good." He reached under the flap of the covered basket and retrieved a tall, black candle. The candle was placed in the grass before him, and with his cane he tapped four spots in the dirt over and around it. "Take your candles, set them there. Make a border."

The boys obliged. Once the candles were in place, Victor stood above them and, with his cane hovering inches above the earth, slowly traced a perimeter between the five points, mapping out an invisible wide-topped pentagon. The shape, if drawn, would be a little over a foot wide, and it seemed to Karel that Victor seemed less interested in the phantom perimeter than he was the blank space inside. The older boy looked into the space and spoke to Lyonel.

"You brought matches."

Lyonel nodded, and checked his pockets — empty. Fritz withdrew his companion's matchbook from his own breast pocket.

Victor took the matches. He withdrew one and, with an exaggerated flick of his wrist, set it ablaze. The flames danced across his soft, gray eyes which glinted like cold marble. He lowered the match to his candle, then made his way to the others, each newly lit monolith emitting a warm crackling glow. When they were all alight, Victor returned to the basket and tapped his cane against its side.

"You're wondering what's in here," he said, retrieving a curved pipe from his pocket and stuffing it with rank tobacco. "Before I share, I have a story, a very strange story, about something that happened last night."

Victor lit his pipe, snuffed the match, and took a long, theatrical puff. Max scoffed, and his leader began:

"It was late in the evening — Father had dismissed the servants and took his flask to bed. I finished reading a slim volume of morbid verse, and upon closing the book I found my head swarmed with strange notions and unusual sentiments. So, I crept undetected out from my chamber, down the spiral stairs, to the kitchen whose door opened out to the garden. The servants locked it earlier, but I always keep a key." Here, he tapped a finger against the hollow head of his cane. "So in spite of Father's draconian curfew, I unlocked the door and stepped outside.

"I should mention, as I'm loath to disrespect her memory, that the garden was my mother's, and she cared for it impeccably. When I was a boy I would often join her in tending the crop, and I spent many summer afternoons playing among thick-stemmed tomato plants, picking from bushels of shining blackberries. Nowadays, the servants tend the garden, and they do a poor job of it — it's not unusual to find clumps of yellowed weeds or the corpse of some malnourished bushel. Still, I'm grateful for their effort, as merely being in the garden gives me a nostalgic comfort and, on certain special nights when gripped by fits of heightened sensitivity, an unquantifiable sense of peace.

"Last night was no different — the moment I stepped into the garden the turbulence about my head mellowed into something vaguely decipherable. A crisp and cold air, not unlike tonight's, rustled the thick-leafed plants with a gentle breeze, underscoring the songs of chirping crickets. Waiting for my thoughts to form, I smoked my pipe and watched the moon — the moon which, quite as it is now, seemed sharp and severe like the sickle of some celestial reaper, poised for an imminent harvest. I looked and thought and smoked, and everything felt right, everything was good.

"Yet I was so mired in thought that it was only when my pipe burned low that I noticed the change in atmosphere: gone was the breeze, gone the insect chorus. All I heard, besides the workings of my breath, was a low, worming whistle. It came from somewhere deeper in the garden. So I drew towards it, slowly, past rows of wilting blossoms and between bent stalks. I began to hear, alongside the whistling, the faint flapping of wings — flappings racing like a thumping heart. And it was only when I reached the shriveled sunflowers that I saw…"

Victor trailed off, eyes darting across his puzzled audience. He continued:

"I saw there was some *thing*," he said, stressing the word, "fat and pale, an oblong body, two pudgy arms, two pudgy legs, a big round head. Almost like a baby. And larger than it should've been. It was looking right into the face of a dead sunflower and fluttering on wings that shone like sun-struck glass. And it was glowing dimly blue. I snuck closer behind it and saw that the dim blue glow did not come from its pale skin, but from *beneath* its skin, as if its flesh was nothing more than a lantern's shade. So I crept behind the thing as it studied the corpse, and as I rose from my crouch, I held my cane high…" Victor demonstrated, curling back his arm and holding his instrument like a cudgel, "and as it began to turn… I swung—!"

The cane slammed into the dirt; Fritz jumped. Victor grinned, a saw-tooth twinkle in his eye.

"The thing fell hard. Its wings were twitching like insect legs, so I hit them until they stopped. And then the thing was still — moaning, but still. So I came back with black tarp, wrapped it up, and took it inside. And so I've kept it."

It took a moment for the boys to realize that was where the story ended. Victor lounged like a sphynx on his cane, surveying the crowd. He caught Karel staring.

"Well?" Victor asked.

Karel turned his eyes to the depths of night.

Lyonel chuckled. "You were right. It is strange. Honestly, I don't—"

"*Strange*," Max spat the word as a curse. "Sure — it's all made up. It's horseshit. It's a joke on us. Because he's great, and clever, and we're stupid, and we listened."

Victor laughed, but did not respond. Instead he reached inside the basket and retrieved a black bundle. The bundle was bound tightly in twine, and when Victor stepped towards the assembled candles, Karel could've sworn he saw it shudder. Victor placed the bundle in the center of the phantom pentagon and withdrew his pair of long-bladed scissors. He held the blades aloft, snipped them in the air for show, and stuck their open beak around the bundle's center knot. He paused, raised an open hand.

"Look," he said.

The twine was cut and the sack unwound. Like a black flower at dawn the folds blossomed outwards, and there in the shadowy iris was a skinned creature splayed out on its side. The miserable lump did in fact glow, however, contrary to what Victor had described, the poor thing's body was not illumined by some inner light but rather by the five candles whose flames flickered across its flayed, bloody body.

*It must be an animal*, Karel thought, *it must be something natural*, though nothing with a body like that had wings like those — a fowl's wings, nearly picked clean, only a few feathers still stuck to mangled bone. One of the wings twitched, the other didn't, and both were broken so horribly as to be beyond salvation.

The thing had degraded, spoiled somehow. Victor had beaten it, yes, but not skinned it, not plucked its glassy wings. He first thought it was dead and in the process of a remarkably swift decomposition, but the twitching proved otherwise. Its ruined head spasmed, jerking on a fractured neck. The upper lefthand corner of its skull was deflated, torn muscle sunk into a soft crater. The head had no eyes to speak of, but it retained a mouth — a gaping, elliptical mouth rimmed by a halo of crusted blood. The mouth moved slowly, wheezing, a gurgled parody of its worming whistle. In the dim light afforded by the candles, Fritz could see the trembling of small, stained teeth within the shade, and he sobbed into Lyonel's chest.

"God," Max muttered as he sank to the ground. "God. What is it?"

Karel thought of an answer amidst warped phantoms of spires and saints, yet dared not speak.

"New territory," Victor blurted, composure hastily mended. "Nothing you've ever seen on Earth. And it's here — I brought it here, just for us."

"What do you want us to do with it?" Lyonel asked.

"What all scientists, all curious men of the world must do with something new. We will take it apart to see how it works." The boys looked in disbelief. Their candles were halfway gone, and the high-rising fog formed an enclosed room around them, trapping them with the thing, and with their leader.

"Come, you are men, yes? Surely you don't think I've just brought you here for fun? You're here to learn. We're all here to learn. And we're not going to learn merely by tasting the vices of adults — we're going to do as they do, overcome their knowledge on their terms. Think of it like biology, when we cut open a sheep fetus or a stinking cow's head. Only this time there is no map, and what we find will be entirely unspoiled by precedent."

"But the sheep and the cows…" Lyonel trailed off. "This thing is alive."

"It is. And we'll see for how much longer. Now — your scissors."

With trembling hands, Max and Lyonel retrieved their blades, and Lyonel, seeing as Fritz would hardly move, took his pair and shoved it in the grip of the quivering boy. Then only Karel was empty-handed. He hadn't moved or said a word since the creature was unveiled. He only watched it as he would a passing cloud, and he'd yet to feel a reason to do anything else. He didn't see everyone stare.

"Karel," Victor snapped. "The scissors."

Karel's breath hitched.

Max laughed: "It's that thing. It must remind him of his sister."

Karel lurched across the field, kicked over a candle, now-drawn

## LONG SCISSORS, BLACK CANDLES

scissors flashing in the dim light as he held them like a knife before Max's throat. Max could only sit, Karel just stood. The blade wavered in his hand.

"Karel," Victor said. Karel didn't move. "Karel, listen to—"

The skinned thing screamed. Its whole body spasmed as if struck by a sudden seizure, hollow bones snapping as it rolled around in the dirt. Max fell back and struck the foot of the throne. Karel dropped the blade, and the screaming died as Victor stomped the creature's face into earth.

Karel ran. Nobody watched. The grassy meadow gave way to

patchy, uneven dirt, and the boy began to stumble over stray rocks and upturned roots. He barreled through the forest unfolding its edges across the dim fog, a confusion of jagged lines. As long as he ran, the thin halo of woodland seemed to bend and stretch out past its natural limits, coiling back into a labyrinth nestled within some foggy infinity.

And it was from the depths of that foggy infinity that the whistle first blew, rattling the trelliswork of jagged branches above. The sound shot Karel's nerves and dragged him to a halt. He leaned against a tree and listened. The whistle sounded again — louder, closer, an unearthly sound vibrating through the trees and the grass and the tips of his quivering fingers. In the depths of the abyss, Karel saw the shimmerings of a faint blue orb, the gleaming of a cold star.

As the whistling grew nearer, the glow grew brighter, and Karel could see that the light was not alone — its pale blue shimmer was contained in the stomach of what appeared to be a triangular glass lantern. The glow was completely unsupported and seemed to come from nowhere — like a large, unwavering firefly, hovering calmly in the center of its containment. And that containment, topped with a large metal ring, was held in a long-fingered hand which now emerged from a curling wall of mist.

The hand was all the flesh it had. The wrist, and anything beyond, was swallowed in a yawning sleeve which hung limp around invisible upholstery, long and crooked like a grasshopper's leg. The thing was all tatters; tall even with its hunch, the byproduct of a pair of long, bulging lumps that twitched and tittered beneath covered shoulders. Its face, what little Karel could see beyond its hood, was night and nothing more. He retreated behind the tree.

Curling into a ball, the boy pressed himself against the trunk. He shut his eyes and covered his ears. It was no use — the whistle which doubtlessly spilled forth beyond the heavy hood, could not be quieted, and Karel recognized in the total darkness behind his eyelids the void of the shrouded face. Twigs crackled, the whistling blared, the dry branches above shook as if battered by heavy winds. Karel knew his only escape was down the hill, in the village, in the house where his mother and father might be waiting. He didn't notice that the whistling had stopped nor that he was crying.

Four screams punctured the night. The cries peaked in the distance and rose like wisps of smoke, echoing across the now-

## LONG SCISSORS, BLACK CANDLES

cleared forest up into the starry vault. Karel craned up towards the screams, and what he saw he could hardly comprehend. The tattered figure was walking among the stars. The lump on its back had sprouted — two raven-black wings now flapped freely, and the train of its worn fabric undulated softly in the air. Its lantern was fastened to a belt on its waist, and both of its hands were full. With one the tattered figure cradled the mangled corpse of the skinned thing against its shoulder like an infant; with the other it led an unusual procession. Four figures trailed behind the tatters in a chain of linked hands — the first was Victor, who held Max, who held Lyonel, who in turn held Fritz. They all cried.

The procession shrunk as it climbed to the shining blade of the moon, and soon the wailing was lost behind the calls of crickets and the softest rustling of Autumn winds.

All that remained was the pale speck of the lantern's glow, which twinkled once before vanishing completely.

# PATIENCE IS THE VIRTUE
## AIMEE OGDEN

HOWARD OFTEN REMINDS CAROLINE that she owes him her gratitude. Though her face cannot possibly betray her inner thoughts, he reads into the perfect composition of her expression as he likes. In the mornings, after the maid has lit the lamps, dressed Caroline, combed and pinned her hair, and settled her into place at the breakfast table, Howard observes in his wife a quiet dignity, a peaceful acceptance of her life. In the evenings, his comportment becomes solicitous: she must be tired, he says, what a long day. Only at night, while Caroline stares unblinking at the ceiling and his own repose is not forthcoming, does he find her cold and ungrateful. "I have made you immortal," he tells her. "Any other woman would be glad of that gift."

Sometimes that is enough for him to roll over and fall asleep beside her, the slope of his shoulder leaving a long dark stain at the periphery of her sight. Sometimes he makes her counterargument for her. "I suppose you will say you were not consulted in the matter. But it is for the head of household to make difficult decisions such as this one. And perhaps you feel that it is an imperfect sort of immortality — well, of course it is! But my God, Caroline, surely you can see the advantage when compared against the alternative."

She cannot see it, and she cannot respond. Eventually, his double-stranded argument unwinds itself into sleep. Caroline remains awake, long after his rest settles upon him, and wakes before him too. She is most at peace then, before the dawn, when her eyes have dried out and stranded her in a dark, half-painted world.

∼

The simulacrum of herself, inside which the great Dr. Howard Irving has placed her, appears as the normal human form to all but the most discerning scientific eye. There are no nerves in her body, no muscles to strain against bone. The skeleton is there, to forge shape from void, and to house the few parts carried over from her dying body: her brain, her eyes, the delicate workings of her inner ear. This last demanded the most precision in the transfer, Howard has explained; but he could not bear the thought of depriving her of her husband's voice across the coming years. Because he is a man, the stronger sex, he has the capacity to tolerate the remainder of his mortal life without hearing her speak again.

Her skin now is starched silk, dyed to a healthy pinkish complexion and painstakingly spotted with the same constellations of freckles that marked her in life. To lend depth to her skeletal form, Howard has hand-sewn silk bags to exacting proportion and stuffed them with sawdust. Her waist draws in narrower now than it did in life, Howard sometimes points out, in keeping with the new fashion, now that she need not manage the difficulties of digestive organs.

She must be kept away from the windows, and cannot be perambulated through the garden in her wheelchair, lest the sun's harsh rays unmake what her husband has made. To her, this would be no great sacrifice; she would like to see the sun again, and the green world all around. But her opinion goes unspoken and unheard.

Though she has no stomach, her preserved brain requires a carbohydrate substrate to maintain itself — the immortality with which she has been fitted is less than perfect on that account. Each morning the maid must move her from her bed to a cart, upon which she is transferred to the specially-built service elevator. It creaks down past the levels of the house — the bedrooms, the sitting and dining rooms — and deposits itself in Dr. Irving's shadow-strewn cellar workshop.

There, the maid strips her to her false skin and submerges her in a nutrient bath. Caroline remains there, beneath the surface, for thirty minutes, to stare at nothing through the murky grayish liquid. Finally she is removed again, to be dried and dressed and properly coiffed. Only then can the day's breakfast be served. Dr. Irving is particular about how his poached egg is presented.

Despite this forced proximity, the hired girl is careful never to meet Caroline's eyes. As she is dragged into or out of the bath, Caroline sees whatever is in front of her; chiefly the discarded remains of previous experiments. The maid refuses to clean the workshop, a fact which Howard only accepts because he fears what mess an unschooled girl may make of his equipment far more than he abhors her disobedience.

Beside Howard's operating table, a glassy-eyed, hollow dog, desiccated for want of its own nutrient bath, lies on its side. Its legs stand out at dire angles, thanks to its haphazard stuffing and mounting. In another corner is a pig, its eyes horrible and human, deflated where its manmade muscles have been reclaimed and repurposed. Worst of all is the puddle of a creature, shoved under a cupboard, not even provided with its own bones upon which to hang its shallow little life. This last appears mammalian like the rest, but beyond that offers no clues as to its nature or provenance.

These curiosities were being constructed and disassembled under Caroline's own roof, while she was too ill to rise from her deathbed. Before that, perhaps; there were questions she did not ask and arguments she did not start, even when it was within her power to do so.

The maid whispers the Lord's Prayer under her breath, over and over again, until the bath is over and they can leave the cellar again. Howard hired her on the basis of her reputation for discretion; whatever horrors have been pressed upon her in this house, she saves them for the Virgin's ears alone. If she would just meet Caroline's eye, Caroline would try to speak to her, with that look. *They cannot hurt us*, she wants to tell the girl. *I cannot hurt you. It's all right.*

But the girl does not meet Caroline's eye, and anyway, it is certainly not all right.

~

Because of the silk and the sawdust, Caroline is soft, as a woman is meant to be. At least, without the input of flesh and muscle and nerve, she feels nothing when her husband heaves himself atop her. From her vantage, she cannot tell what sort of receptive apparatus, if any, he has fitted to her. Whatever mark he leaves on her, whatever stain — everything dissolves in the nutrient bath, one way or another.

When he is finished, he rolls off and gives a deep sigh. "It's a pity," he often says. "That we never had children — before."

∽

Her brother comes to lunch on a Saturday afternoon. He and Dr. Irving have much to discuss: the characteristics of this year's influenza, the North Pole, something about monkeys on trial in Tennessee. Hardly any of it scratches the ill-polished veneer of Caroline's understanding. Howard never speaks to her of such things, and when he sits beside her on the settee, he insists on tuning the radio to something frivolous and frothy. The Waldorf-Astoria Orchestra and the Eveready Hour better suit a housewife's tender temperament than weighty politics or shocking world news.

The maid sets out the meal in the French service style: a roast, weeping juices onto its platter; tureens of oxtail soup; rice pudding with an ominous greasy sheen on top. There is a plate in front of Caroline, too, and Howard serves her a generous slice of beef, a stuffed egg, a mound of pudding that immediately calves off into several smaller piles. While the men eat, the maid unobtrusively clears Caroline's meal. Though her brother takes no notice, Howard watches the maid's every movement, following her with his eyes until she leaves the room behind the serving-cart.

When the conversation has wound down and the plates have been cleaned, her brother turns to her and tilts his head seriously. "You've been quiet, Caddie dear. Are you still unwell?"

"The illness has left her quite exhausted," says Howard. His hand envelops her elbow: she cannot feel it, but she can see its shadow. "You must forgive her any reticence."

"Of course, of course!" As he rises from the table, her brother presses a kiss upon Caroline's forehead, and turns to follow Dr. Irving into his office for a sip of brandy.

When the men have gone, the maid returns to clear. She eats the scraps out of the rice-pudding bowl first, scraping the spoon against the sides, then lifts Dr. Irving's tureen of oxtail soup to tip the dregs into her mouth. As she sets the empty bowl on the serving-cart, she catches Caroline's eye, and gasps.

*It's all right*, Caroline tries to say, with her eyes. *You ought to eat for both of us. Tell me how it tastes, and if it is vile, lie to me.*

It is as if, for the first time, the girl recognizes that there is a person inside Caroline's stiff, indifferent form — and she recoils from it. She abandons the cart and bustles Caroline into her wheelchair, hurrying her into the service elevator and abandoning her beside the writing-desk in the bedroom. Before she leaves, she draws the curtains imperfectly shut. A single line of sunset pink shines through the gap, and it burns a white bar across Caroline's sight.

∼

Three times a day, the maid comes to put moistening drops in Caroline's eyes. A routine made mechanical by its frequency; yet today, the girl's hand trembles on Caroline's chin, and false tear-tracks paint themselves down Caroline's cheeks.

She cannot feel them, but with her head pulled toward the maid, she can see the pitter-patter of raindrops that they leave on the skirt of her day dress. There is oil in the solution, to keep it from drying too quickly; likely these drops will stain.

Caroline doesn't mind the stains — who would notice them? Only the maid, who will be tasked with the laundry anyway. She cannot cry on her own, and she is only grateful that someone else has helped her to do it.

∼

The thump shudders through the wall and into the bed, jarring Caroline awake.

The bedroom is dark: lamps extinguished for the night, stars unable to pierce the damask curtains. Though Caroline cannot blink to clear her sight, she thinks the lightless mountain of Howard's side is absent.

A deep, muffled voice fails to penetrate the bedroom wall. Howard is in the hallway outside, but to whom is he speaking? The wall reverberates with an unseen strike, vibrating the headboard. Perhaps Caroline ought to be afraid; but then again, she thinks, fear

**PATIENCE IS THE VIRTUE**

would require a body, to sweat and tremble, a heart to thunder against the underside of real muscle and flesh. Because she lacks the machinery to manufacture fear, she manages a dull curiosity. Patience is the virtue inscribed deep in every moment of her existence.

More blows, one by one, but they grow fainter, until they fade away altogether. Then a blunted silence. Morning still has not arrived to throw back the night's curtains, but Caroline does not suppose she will sink back into sleep before it does.

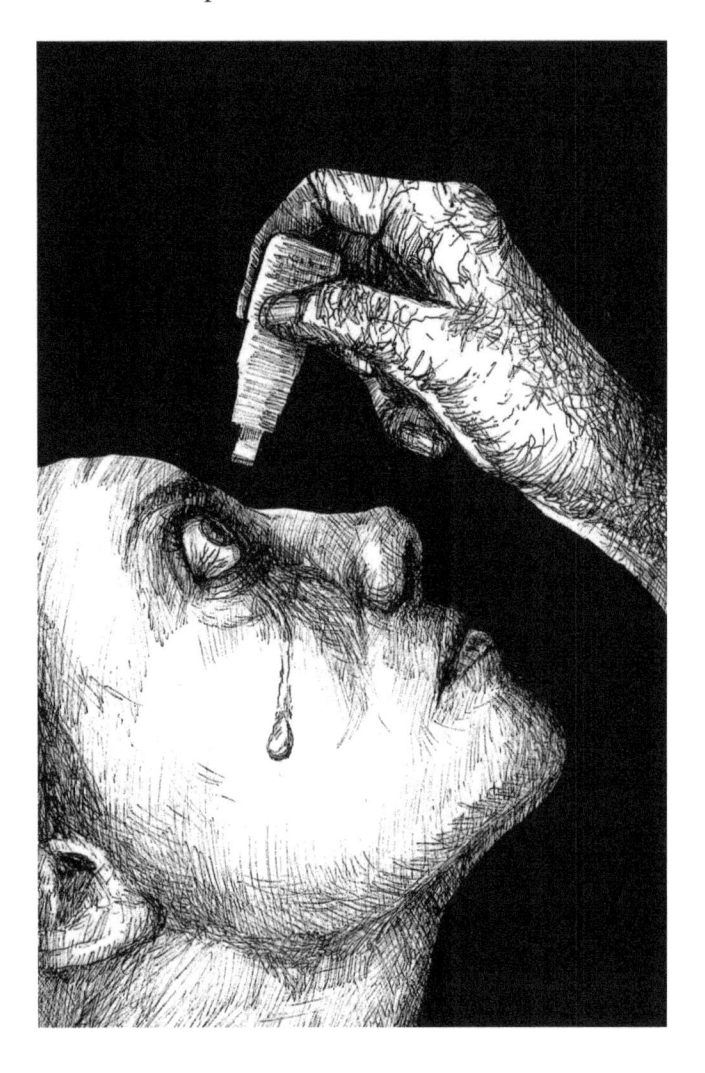

The bedroom door crashes open. A flash of gold and white breaks through the darkness, framed by the light in the hall outside. The shape is too slight to belong to Howard. Without light — or the needed drops for her eyes — Caroline can only assume that this must be the maid, in her nightdress, her long hair unbound.

The girl hurries across the room on mousy little footfalls, but a sob breaks out of her before she reaches the dresser. She weeps, big ugly gulping cries, half-retching, as she slams the drawers open to their limits and upsets the tidy rows of Caroline's jewelry. Necklaces tinkle softly as she sweeps them together; bracelets complain more loudly of their rough treatment.

By the time the girl has finished ransacking the jewelry dresser, she has calmed — or at least quieted. She turns toward Caroline, edging closer to the bed, without coming within what would once have been Caroline's reach. Her face is a pink blur with two dark hollows where her eyes should be. The front of her nightdress bears dark blotches that, in the dark, do not admit of their true color.

The maid draws one more shallow, shuddering breath. The stolen jewelry jingles as she rustles around, seeking something on her person. Caroline cannot tell what that something is, until a cheerful little scrape brings to life a small, bright blotch of pale yellow. The brightness dances. It wavers.

With her eyes, Caroline tries to speak to the maid. *Yes*, she says; only that. *Yes*. She puts every ounce of affirmation that she can into her dry, motionless stare. *Yes. Yes. Yes.*

The match head hovers a moment more. Then it arcs through the air, out of Caroline's sight. A soft whoosh, and a column of light crawls up her periphery, beside where the window would be. The maid's retreating footsteps are lost behind the mounting chorus of merry crackling. Caroline wishes she could thank the girl, too, but she is smart to flee quickly, lest she breathe too much smoke, and take ill, and fall under the interested eye of a man who would like to save her. The jewelry ought to buy her a better life than that; but then, those dainty sparkling things hadn't been enough to spare Caroline.

The light creeps tenderly up over the bedcovers, sliding over Caroline's legs. She cannot feel it, but she sees the ring of white that embraces her. The brightness grows in magnitude, in nearness, the circle of dark melting away before its advance. Before it closes in upon her, before there is a stillness inside to match the one outside, her world is a sun that never surrenders to its horizon.

# HELLO

## JOHN PATRICK HIGGINS

"HELLO. HOW MUCH FOR THE PHONE?"

The young woman running the stall barely looked up.

"There's a sticker," she said.

The sticker was on the underside of the phone, so I had to hold the receiver in the cradle to look at it. A little yellow sticker from a pricing-gun like you'd get in Londis, but the price was handwritten in biro. She wanted fifty quid for it.

"Fifty quid?"

This has happened all over. You used to be able to get actual bargains sifting through second-hand shops and markets. People bought by weight; they never knew what they had. Now the market value of any given thing is a Google search away. Today there are no bargains. Still, fifty pounds for an old phone was steep.

"You can get rotary phones new on Amazon for that," I said.

She looked up but she didn't get up. She had pink hair and pink glasses, both the frames and lenses. She tilted her head, looking at me from under a jagged fringe.

"That's a proper phone. Feel the weight of it. The smell of it. There's nothing like old Bakelite. That mouthpiece smells of cigarettes, dentures, discontinued lipsticks. It's heavy with the weight of years. People have been telling it their secrets for a century. You can't get that on Amazon."

It was quite a good pitch, I had to admit.
"I'll give you twenty-five."
"All right."

I took the phone into the cinema with me. She didn't have any carrier bags. I thought for a moment about buying a tote bag with a Medieval woodcut of a witch naming her familiars on it, but instead I sat the phone on my lap as I watched Bava's *Black Sabbath*.

∼

The phone sat on my hall table the way phones used to. It was black and heavy, gloomy as a doctor's bag. The plastic of the dial had yellowed with age, a tobacco taint, and I wondered about the previous owner's carrot-coloured digits digging into its holes. It looked great: strong and sturdy, a receiver you could have brained someone with. Like Batman's landline.

It was purely decorative. I hadn't plumbed it in, or anything. I thought I might do one day but for now it was just a nice thing to have in the house. I have a lot of old things. I prefer them. Design was sexier in the past. Things are functional now: bland, ergonomically smooth, sharp edges shaved off. I prefer the panache of the past: big, clunky boxes of stuff, built by hands for hands. Chunky buttons with feel appeal, and a whole range of colours. Everything's so dull now. This is the age of oatmeal. I expect the reason is the destruction of the planet. Our cars are boring, our children rarely out of our sight, their phones tapped and tracked, because TV news continually tells us everything outside is howling chaos. The animals are dying, the ice caps melting, Russia is threatening nuclear strikes on its neighbours, currencies collapse and the politicians we elect — when we get to vote for them at all — are venal idiots, clawing up the culture. Billionaires are stealing and sitting on all the money in the world, before flying into space with it. That's how we live now. So, we hide in our boring houses, cosseting our doomed children who can't cope.

Maybe I'm being sentimental, preferring the things of the past. It's a moral cowardice hiding there, a time when the planet still had a chance. The mid-twentieth Century, when the only thing we were destroying was each other.

I'd been to the Supermarket, wheeling the trolley around one-handed with practiced ease. I could handle a shopping trolley, oh yes. But the shop was rammed, and people got in my way. They would stand, trolleys parallel to the produce pondering their purchases, meaning I couldn't get near any food. I returned to the car park to find myself boxed in by a Land Rover and waited until a jolly middle-aged woman in a gilet returned with a bottle of Prosecco.

"Sorry, thought I'd only be five minutes."

She shrugged and climbed into her car. I didn't know people still wore gilets.

I was fuming when I got home, trying to negotiate the door-lock with two shopping bags in my hands. I was stressed, and the noise was just another annoyance, so I didn't think. When the phone rang, I picked it up, pressing the black receiver to my mouth in a way that felt entirely natural.

"Hello?"

Then I dropped the receiver. Because I recognised the voice. Though I hadn't heard that voice for twenty-five years.

I knew it.

I picked up the receiver again.

"Hello?"

"What are you playing at?" said the impossible voice. It sounded exactly as it had done two decades ago.

"Sophie?"

"Of course, Sophie," said the voice, "Who else would be ringing you? No one else likes you."

"I didn't think you did," I said.

"You're all right."

"Why're you ringing me after all this time?" My voice squeaked. I was having heart palpitations. "I mean, it's nice to hear from you and everything — you haven't changed a bit — but it's a bit out of the blue. How've you been? What've you been up to? God."

A sigh fell through the black hole of the receiver. Her breath in my ear. "This isn't that funny, actually."

"I don't understand." This was an accurate statement. I was standing in my hallway surrounded by bags of shopping, chatting to my ex-girlfriend on a phone that was unconnected to a phone line. The front door was still open, key in the lock.

"Okay, this got very boring very quickly. Ring me when you're in the mood to talk properly."

She rang off. No dialling tone. A click and silence. I braced myself against the banister, eyes blurring, throat tight with the shock. That *was* her. That was Sophie. That, impossibly, was her voice, exactly as I remembered it. A young voice, a girlish voice. Sophie would be fifty now. But the things she said and the way she said them: it *was* her. But it couldn't have been. Sophie, even thirty years ago, was not the sort of person to ring you and pretend to have just spoken to you if she hadn't. And what was the point? As a prank it didn't work — she'd given up far too quickly. It didn't go anywhere. Freaking someone out wasn't funny on its own, and that's all she'd done. But the oddest thing, really the strangest thing, was that the phone call could never have taken place — the phone didn't work.

I lifted the receiver again. Silence. Because there had to be. The phone was just a dumb lump of Bakelite squatting on my hall table. Decoration. I replaced the phone onto the cradle and closed the front door, taking the bags of shopping into the kitchen, my hands shaking through the thin plastic handles.

Sophie was my first girlfriend. She was a serious person, and I was not a very serious person, and I thought that made us a great match. After three years she disagreed and dumped me. It was only at that point I realised I loved her, achingly and hopelessly. I knew suddenly that I would always love her and love no one else but her for the rest of my life. I told her this in a series of increasingly desperate letters, as she no longer answered my calls. Later her mother told me she'd got a job in London. I moved on to a short-lived romance with a girl I didn't much like. It ended badly. I never heard from Sophie again, so you can understand my confusion when she rang me out of the blue after a quarter century's silence.

Over the next few days whenever I walked through the hallway, I would snatch up the phone to check the dial tone wasn't there. I never caught it out. I also tried to track down Sophie on social media. I'm going to insist this was not creepy. I'd had a very strange experience, and I was trying to find if there was the possibility of it really being her, or perhaps a daughter who sounded like her and was playing a joke on me for some reason. Perhaps I was still remembered as a figure of fun in Sophie's house — Mum's first idiot boyfriend. God.

But I could find nothing — we had no shared friends on social media, and beyond that, well, my technical skills are limited. Nothing else happened, and the phone continued to sit on the hall table, gathering dust. I stopped noticing it. I had newer toys to play with. I'd found this incredible demilune walnut astragal glazed display cabinet at an auction in the middle of nowhere. Got it for a song. Slight foxing on the interior lining but otherwise not a scratch on it. It sits regally in my living room, begging me to stuff it with further *objets de tat*, and I'm powerless before its luminous beauty.

I was down the stairs and still fuddled with sleep before I realised. My mobile was charging on my bedside table, as it did every night. That was not the phone that was ringing. The house was black. I felt for the light switch while the phone continued ringing, and the hall snapped into stark, pitiless light, the room taking on a sudden, sterile quality. It felt less like light had been added, more the darkness had been erased. I looked at the fat black phone, and in a breathless moment picked up the receiver, pressing it to my ear.

"All right?"

The voice was light, adenoidal, the inflection more affirmative than questioning. This was a greeting rather than a question about my wellbeing. It was what we said. I knew the voice immediately. It was three in the morning, and I was on the phone to my childhood friend, Alan.

"Alan?"

"No mate, this is Prince out of "Prince and the Revolution." We was wonderin' if you'd finished with our linen? Only we got a lot of lacey collars and cuffs and that, and we need our washing done. I got burger juice on me cravat."

It was Alan, all right. I missed Alan. He was a silly bastard, but he was okay. But how could I miss him? He was talking to me right now on the phone. The same boy I'd known all those years ago.

"Bloody hell. Alan."

"What gave me away? How did you see through my subterfuge?"

"Where are you ringing from, mate?" I tried to sound casual, pitching my voice up to match his.

"My mum's. Where I'm always calling from."

"Yeah, what's the number. I think I've lost that number." He gave me his mum's number, and I wrote it down, knowing when I rang it, I would hear the voice of a confused old woman. There was no way of calling him back. The phone didn't work. It wasn't connected.

"What have you been up to, mate?"

He told me. It was amazing how boring his life was. A teenage boy, living with his parents, a virgin boy, and likely to stay one a long time. He went to school, and he came home. He ate beans on toast in front of the TV. That was Alan's life. Mine too. We had nothing to talk about, we'd seen each other at school that day, and yet he rang me most evenings with banal gossip, breathlessly related. It was so strange. I wondered whether this conversation, any of these conversations, had really taken place. Whether, in 1984 or 5, my friend Alan had rung what he thought was his friend, and had spoken to a man in his fifties, pretending to be his mate. Did I sound 14 to him? Neither he nor Sophie seemed to notice the difference. Were they hearing the voice they expected to hear? I didn't know what was happening, I didn't know how, and I didn't know why. But I wanted it to carry on. I was living for these phone calls, strange postcards from a distant star. I hated going to work in case I missed one. I hated sleeping or going out and meeting people. I moved my armchair into the hall so I could sit there in comfort. I couldn't move the phone into the living room. It had to stay where it was, where the magic first started to happen. I had no explanation for why the calls came through, but they first came through on the phone in the hallway, so that was the position they had to stay in. I couldn't break the spell. I didn't know why it worked there but it did and possibly only there, so there it would stay. I had no means to fix the broken magic if I broke it. The armchair lived in the hall, and I sat there each night. Sometimes I slept there.

When a call finished, I would quickly write everything I remembered about it: who was calling, how they'd sounded and what they said. I noted what time it had been when they rang, what their relationship was to me or my family. Occasionally the caller did not want to talk to me but to my parents, and that seemed like a big clue. I began to see patterns even as the calls diminished in frequency. There were builders, butchers, family friends, representatives of my school, childhood and teenage friends, but nothing after I left home at 18. The calls were randomly dotted through a ten-year period. The content of the conversations seemed immaterial or inconclusive. Some were banal: cold callers, my parent's laundry, representatives of governmental bodies, a dental receptionist cancelling an appointment for a filling (I feigned joy, and she sharply advised me that I couldn't delay the inevitable). Others had a meaning now they didn't then: the voices of friends like Alan, who had died at twenty-three in a car crash. My uncle Bill, a fun uncle I'd loved growing up and whose funeral I'd missed because I'd been at university and couldn't afford the train fare. I was dumped at least three times over the phone. I remembered crying at the time and was pleased my replies were far more phlegmatic this time around, to the point that my angry girlfriend started crying and asked me why I didn't care. It felt like revenge. I was so cruelly civil.

And that was the strange thing: my responses to these calls were not the same as I remembered them. They couldn't have been. I said different things which in turn forced different responses from the other end of the line. Sometimes the changes were subtle, a speech inflection, details I'd forgotten, as most of the chats related to minor events from thirty years before. Other times conversations were utterly transformed.

A PE teacher from my school rang to complain about me to my parents. Mr Fox was a nasty piece of work, a shower-room dawdler with a lank moustache and sad, weary eyes. He was five-foot five and whippet thin, wore Rugby shirts and drove a sports car with a rusted exhaust, farting his noxious clouds past the bus queue. He was a needling bully with a long memory, and he wanted to speak to my parents.

"Harry? It's Mr Fox. I need to speak to your mum and dad."

"They're not here."

"Not here *Mr Fox*. How very convenient. When will they be back?"

"Don't know."

"Are you lying to me? Because if I find they *are* in fact at home, and you've been giving me some spurious snow job, I'll be down on you like a ton of bricks."

I'd forgotten he did that — littered sentences with words like "spurious" to make himself sound clever. As a PE teacher, he may have been insecure. He had every reason to be.

"I doubt you'd do that, sir."

"Do you indeed, young Harry? You might want to be careful about what you say to me."

"The ton of bricks part, sir," I said, "you're what? Nine stone? I reckon my mum could take you if it came down to it."

A brief silence.

"My office, tomorrow. You'll be picking up leaves from the sports ground in the pissing rain for three hours, son. That's what I think of back-chat."

"You're a sad, little confused man, Craig," I said, "standing by the showers clocking those hairless little pricks dancing in and out of the water. Cracking on to the fifth form girls, cruising the bus queue in your shitty little two-seater. This is it for you. You're stuck at that school. I'll leave. I'll go off and do whatever it is I'm going to do, and you'll still be there, greying to powder and avoiding parent's evening, because all the kids you were a bastard to will come back and see you're still there, like an insect trapped in amber, powerless to free yourself."

There was a long, heavy sigh from the other end of the phone, then a click. He'd hung up. He'd just hung up. I was enervated, my breathing heavy, unable to stop giggling. I'd got him back. I'd told him what I thought. After all this time. Was that what this was for? Revenge? Served cool and remote but offering final closure. I couldn't shake the feeling that there should be more consequences, that I should remember more fall-out from these conversations. I would never have said it at the time. It would have been unthinkable, but Foxy really thought he was talking to me. There would have been repercussions — you didn't talk to authority figures like that in those days or, certainly, I didn't. I was a good boy. And a coward. Foxy knew that, and he knew my parents were shy and non-confrontational. They would have believed my teacher over me every time, that was how it was then. They would have punished me, and Fox would have punished me. But nobody had done. At least not that I could remember. Perhaps it was suppressed trauma. Because the calls were real. I was speaking to people from my past. Maybe this was some sort of blissful parallel universe, where I could act with impunity in a consequence free environment. There would be no fall out because how could there be? No one could get me — I lived in the future, far away from any of them. My parents were dead, Mr Fox might well be dead. Alan was dead. I was literally talking to people who were lost forever. I got my notebook out and wrote down everything I remembered Fox and I saying to each other.

∼

My work suffered. My personal relationships, such as they were, suffered too. I was tired all the time. I lost weight and started drinking, just staying in, bored, sat by the phone. There were fewer calls. Or so it seemed, as I was living for them, sitting there each night, notebook on my lap, my pen poised, a tumbler of supermarket own-brand whiskey at my lips.

My parents never rang. That made sense. Why would they? I hoped my dad might, perhaps to say he was staying late at the office, or his train was delayed. The call never came but it was at least possible. I *knew* I'd never hear my mother's voice again. She was a housewife, always at home. She went to the shops and came back again. That was about it for mum. She'd had no discernible social life. Occasionally she and my dad would go out together — fancy dress, a strange new smell, heavy and sweet, an imprint of her lipstick on my cheek, spit-washed off with a Kleenex. The next day the pair of them would be grey and quiet, the radio off in the kitchen, and I knew to retire to my room and draw quietly.

How strangely they lived. Adults, performing their married roles as they knew they should, my mother a virtual anchorite. The only person she saw was me, until I went to school. Then who did she see? Did she meet friends for coffee? Did she do anything that wasn't a kind of drudgery. Later, when I was a teenager, she started to do aerobics, dance classes, anything, celebrating her freedom in her middle years, but it didn't last. She wasn't a joiner. If she'd ever had the knack, she'd lost it during the years of her confinement. My father was the same. They had each other and that was all they had. They clung to one another, and when she died, he withered away in weeks. You'd call it sweet, and maybe it was, but they had no choice. They were victims of their time, of cultural expectation, of their shyness and lack of imagination. They were dull, even in the house, even with each other. The kitchen radio on, but silence between them, a life-long shared silence which was neither contentment nor understanding. It was a blank space where their life should have been. I knew it was unlikely I would ever hear either of their voices again, and I wasn't sure I could remember what they sounded like, they spoke so little. They said nothing.

∼

I was asleep when the phone rang, jarring me into consciousness. The room blinked into light, the frozen light of a lightbulb in the dead of night, seeing your familiar furniture suddenly hard-edged and strange. Pressing the receiver to my ear I knew at once I had been waiting to hear one voice all along, this voice, and this was what the black telephone had been for. It couldn't have been for anything else.

"Hello?"

"Hello. It's you."

I should own up to something now. Probably should have mentioned it before, really. A long time ago I killed someone. Just the one person — it was a mistake. And I got away with it. They were a missing person until they were declared legally dead. I was never even a suspect, which was crazy, but there you go. Never questioned, never hauled up before the judge. Scott free. For years I expected to be caught, and lived my life waiting for the other shoe to drop, watching every breakthrough in DNA testing with morbid fascination. But they had nothing. They had no body. Though I'd been panicked and scared at the time, you would be, I was thorough, and lucky too. The search parties, the reconstructions — some on national television — led to nothing. They were looking in the wrong places.

I'd stopped worrying. In fact, I didn't care. They could arrest me tomorrow and it wouldn't bother me. That's what I've done to my life. It ended on that day as much as hers did. That's a fatuous thing to say, I know. But I haven't been happy a single day since then. I thought I'd give myself away — some subconscious tell would expose me. I'd fuck up the hiding of the body somehow, or I'd let something slip in a drunken moment of sincerity. But I hadn't. Nothing had leaked. I'd killed someone, and I'd done it well. We don't need to get into the details. I don't like to think of them.

As soon as I heard the voice on the phone, I knew this was the end point. I would never hear my parents' voices, or any voice after this call. It had all been leading to this.

Vicky. Her name was Vicky. The girl I killed.

Oh wow. I had her at an advantage. Once again. I was talking to her on the phone thirty years after I'd ended her life, and she had no idea about the nature of our relationship. It was unfair. I'd killed her, murdered her, really. Kill sounds unemotive, like she was livestock or vermin. Killed is just something you do; empathy doesn't come into it. A hitman kills people. It would be wrong to say he murders people. He's a step removed. It's just a job. I *murdered* her, I was a murderer. Her murderer.

I suddenly felt so much, stuff bubbling up I had long suppressed. I was in tears immediately.

"Hello?"

She was starting to sound bored. Her voice was the same. Of course it was, all their voices were the same. You remember voices: voices and smells are the things that stay with you. I'd recognised every one of them over the phone from the first word, a tumult of memories, a flick-book of moments plucked from distant days: a smile, a raised eyebrow, the light in their eyes. A pale body, white against the green, frozen, star shaped.

There was a sigh on the line. I didn't want to lose her.

"Hello."

"Why am I getting the silent treatment?"

"Sorry," I said, "I'm a bit overwhelmed. I'm feeling choked. I'm crying."

"Are you drunk?"

"No. How are you?"

"I'm okay. You okay? You sound weird. You've been a bit off lately."

I remembered how I'd avoided her calls. I'd been playing games, though I don't know if I knew it. I'd reeled her in and shut her out again. She'd been a rebound girlfriend, and she didn't know. She took it all very seriously, too seriously, and I found her so boring. She was confused and I hated her for being confused. I hated her a lot of the time. She'd told me she loved me, and I hated her for that too.

But this was an opportunity. This was a second chance, a chance for redemption. I could shake her off. I could get rid of her. I didn't know when this conversation was taking place, it might even be on

## HELLO

the day. The day I killed her. But if I could put her off now, before the event, I could save her life. I could save her from me. This had to be what the phone was for. This was where it had all been leading. The major event of my life, of her life, could be unpicked. She was being given a second chance just as I was, a chance to cancel out my horrific mistake.

I didn't know how it happened in the first place. It was so out of character. She'd told me she loved me! How did that inspire me to kill her?

I was excited by the possibility of changing the past, of bringing a dead girl back to life. I just needed to break it off, never speak to her again. To ghost her, as they say now.

"I don't want to see you anymore. I never want to see you again."

She said nothing. There was a soft wet sound, like something puncturing flesh.

"Do you understand? I can never see you again. I'm sorry, you have no idea. But you can never come near me again."

I knew immediately I shouldn't have said sorry. It gave her a way in. It implied sorrow on my part or that I was doing this for reasons beyond my control.

"What do you mean sorry? If you're sorry, you don't mean it. I don't believe you."

I had to take back control. I was fighting an implacable foe: my own evil. It seemed ridiculous: a struggle over a damsel in distress, where I was both white knight and dragon. The girl had no purchase on the events over-taking her. She was a seal pup tossed into the air by two sporting orcas. She had no agency at all, as though the young me and the older me had removed her from her own life twice over. And I thought: there is no reason I can't tell her. And that might be the one thing to save her, the only thing to convince her to steer clear of me. I *had* to tell her.

"If you don't stay away from me, if you don't ignore me at all costs, I will kill you, okay? I don't want to kill you, not now, and I'm sorry to say this to you — you have no idea how sorry — but if you don't keep as far from me as possible, I promise you'll die. By my hand. I really mean it. I know I sound mad, but this is because I really want you to live, Vicky. It means everything to me. Please live, okay?"

There was a pause. An electric pause.

"You're fucking crazy."

She hung up. Had it worked? Perhaps. Something still niggled with me, and I wasn't sure what it was. But it was only background noise. I'd got the right result. I'd scared her off. This was amazing. It'd worked. I'd been sufficiently weird on the phone to finally put her off. It must have worked. Why else would I have been given this opportunity? What else could it be for if not to undo the worst thing I ever did, if not to give Vicky back the life I'd robbed her of, a disgusting pointless crime I'd never been punished for and never had the courage to confess to. I felt lighter. I felt liberated. The burden lifted from me. Vicky would live. She would go through life with the memory of me as a dodged bullet, a swerved taxi, something to be shrugged off with a shiver. I'd done it. I knew it. I felt so much better, as though the guilt and the bitterness, the fear of being found out had melted away.

I looked her up on the internet. She was gone. Still missing, presumed dead. Nothing had changed at all. I thought back to the other phone calls, conversations that should have nudged destiny, should have impacted on my life. I should have been spirited to a New York loft or a white sand beach, a cool drink resting on my hard brown belly, or shivering under cardboard in a grey alleyway. Or even failing to exist at all. Slamming down the receiver and winking out of existence for good.

But here I was in my hallway, surrounded by empty bottles, scrolling through my phone looking for news of a dead girl. The calls had taken place in a bubble, there was no causality, and nothing had changed. If I'd given Alan road safety advice, he would still have been mangled in a fatal car crash. The girlfriend who dumped me over the phone would fondly remember my tears, my entreaties, the flex of her power. Foxy never got his comeuppance. Vicky was still dead in a field, scattered white bones in cold dark soil, her life unlived. I'd changed nothing and every call had been a nonsense, a trick played on me.

I picked up the phone and, after feeling its weight in my hand for a moment, hurled it down the hallway. It was too heavy to smash, the receiver flung from the squat black body and snaking across the floor, snapping back on its coiling cord. It was an abject thing. Neck snapped; sinews exposed. Silenced.

I pulled the armchair back into the living room and looked at the chaos my life had become since I'd brought the telephone home. Opening the curtains, I was surprised to meet daylight. I wondered if I still had a job.

I set about cleaning the house. This was it. This was what I could do. I'd failed to sponge the stains from my truncated life, but I would make whatever remained sparkle. I scrubbed on my knees, some needless penance perhaps, a far-too-late corrective. But my new life would shine. The phone had shown me the evils of my past and perhaps I could make reparations in the present. I could turn my life around.

Packing the phone away, I placed the receiver back onto the cradle. It rang. And I knew who it would be on the end of the line and, furthermore, who would always be there on the end of the line. There would be no absolution. No chance to change anything. My past had caught up with me. No redemption. No happy ending.

I picked up the handset.

"Hello?" said a familiar voice.

# THE HAUNTING HOUSE
## DAVID EBENBACH

WHEN THEY FINALLY BUILT A HAUNTED house in our suburban town, we had mixed feelings. On one hand, it was a status symbol, obviously, as it wasn't just any neighborhood that could boast its own haunted house. (Though, to be sure, ours came only after the suburb next to us got one, up in the Heights, a fact that intensified *that* rivalry.) It gave us gravitas, substance, almost even a sense of history. So there was a lot to be excited about. On the other hand, haunted houses are scary.

This one was no exception. Inside a fence made up of what looked like rusty black spears, they had rolled out a thick and tangled lawn, the kind where you wouldn't be able see your own feet as you walked through it. And then, at the end of a path of uneven stone, was the house — dark, Gothically spiky, and every plank and shingle old and unsound. The windows were broken and in some cases hastily boarded up; the others were like empty eye sockets. Everything groaned in the wind. There was even a widow's walk at the top, surrounded by more rusty spears, and in the evenings bats circled the listing chimney. Those bats were good for atmosphere and, we knew, would also help with mosquitos in the summertime.

You could see all of that from the outside. What we couldn't tell, when the contractors' trucks all pulled away, was what was inside. Ghosts were the most likely thing, of course — more or less standard

## THE HAUNTING HOUSE

with this model — but, although vampires tended to prefer places that were in better condition, it was always possible that the designers had installed a down-on-its-luck bloodsucker or two. A deranged slasher in a mask, tormented as a child by peers or parents, was a definite possibility. The property didn't have the acreage to support a werewolf or the water features to sustain a swamp monster, but there was plenty of room for a swarm of human-eating rats or spiders and/or a witch. (Though witches were now a less popular feature as people increasingly realized that that whole concept was just a glaring symptom of the insecure patriarchy. Society does evolve.)

Meanwhile, the rumor was that our rivals in the Heights had, in their haunted house, some kind of ravenous and scientifically perverse space alien.

Of course, this was an important part of the initial experience of the house — the not-knowing. The front door was left slightly open enough to reveal a line of darkness and to bang against the frame in the wind, and not enough to tell us what waited inside.

We speculated about the place, in whispers, for weeks.

And then the house started to announce itself to us. Passing by one evening, Mrs. McCabe heard bursting from a window a noise that sounded to her like a hard laugh. On another occasion, looking from his own porch, Mr. Frazier glimpsed a wavering light in one of the windows — wavering and quickly extinguished. The Nooneys were the first to notice a new smell emanating from the grounds. Decay, perhaps — fresh decay.

And meanwhile the haunted house started to appear in our dreams more or less as soon as construction was complete. The kids first — in the middle of the night, parents told their shaking kids all the usual lies about horrifying things not existing. But those grownups then had to go back to their own cooling beds and contend with their own nightmares. Sometimes we woke up with lingering images of blood or of glowing teeth or with howling still echoing in our ears; other times we resurfaced with vague impressions of helplessness. Mr. Taylor insisted on calling this the *heebie-jeebies*, but it was a great deal more than that. Still — we'd all sometimes had those impressions before the haunted house, too; it was hard to know what was causing what.

Teenagers, ever true to form, were the first to breach the front door.

We had warned our children and one another to stay away. Even the most rationalist among us, the least likely to believe in the supernatural — for example, Mrs. Ballinger was actually *Dr*. Ballinger, a respected chemist, and the Mitchells were both orthopedists — were concerned about crumbling floorboards and tetanus. And everybody knew that serial killers were real. So we issued our warnings. Whether the admonitions slowed down or sped up the teenagers' inevitable steps toward the front door of the house, we can't be sure.

In any case, they entered in little clusters, almost like tour groups. The first, to nobody's surprise, consisted of Angie C. and Jeff L. and their little crew. But they were only the first. All of them picking their way through the grass that seemed to tug at their ankles, climbing up the sagging and gapped front steps, standing on the unsteady porch before the door. They dared each other again and again, silently and aloud, until finally they pushed their way in. Teenagers had been doing this kind of thing for hundreds of thousands of years, and they weren't going to stop now.

They went inside.

Inside, things happened.

What things?

Certainly these young people emerged shaken. Changed. More sober, less certain of themselves, more likely to jump at an unexpected sound or movement. Morgan B., for one, started sleeping with his childhood blankie again, and Tania J. needed a nightlight. This kind of thing was happening all across the neighborhood. Parents pleaded to find out what had happened, exactly — what the kids had seen. But for a long time the teens kept their experiences to themselves, instead staying in their rooms, sitting on their beds, hugging their knees, looking out the windows. Headphones in, but no music, no chatter, no anything.

Finally, though, after much waiting and haranguing, the stories began to be told. Or maybe it was that they began to seep out.

Our younger adolescents tended to describe ghosts. Or *shades* — often the word *shades* was used. And apparently these shades would come out of dark corners and surround their victims, push them back onto creaking, cobwebbed loveseats, and...*talk*. The ghosts of the house were, it seemed, talkers. And what did they have to say? Well,

## THE HAUNTING HOUSE

individual experiences varied somewhat, but certain general themes recurred. The shades talked about the fragility and possibly even meaninglessness of high school love, as well as the likelihood that these adolescents would never grow fully comfortable in their bodies. They painted a picture of sex that was grotesque and desirable and shaming. They told these young people that nobody *really* liked or admired them, and that certainly nobody would ever love them.

The older teens — home from college in many cases — heard a lot about the terrible job market waiting for them after graduation.

Sharing these experiences didn't seem to do any of our adolescents any good; there was no purge, no catharsis. Having been changed by their time in the house, they stayed that way. Removed. Smaller. Hiding behind their blankies.

When the middle-aged people of our suburban town went in next, therefore, they went in angry. It was their kids, after all, who had been haunted. Who now looked into their mirrors with more angst than ever. And so, individually or in pairs — the first were the habitually-bold and chronically-indignant Hadleys, marching toward the house side by side — these parents choked back their fear as much as possible while they ducked swooping bats on the way to the front door, and they opened that front door with chins raised in complaint.

These people, too, came out changed. Back on the outside, they chewed their knuckles raw, fiddled in a manic way with the keys in their pockets, and were often lost in thought. As one typical example, Mr. Folarin's hands had aged markedly. As they went on to tell us — when they eventually found a way to talk about it — they had encountered similar shades, or, more accurately, shades of their own. Because these ones didn't talk about high school, obviously. They talked about the questionable value of work — any work, whether the plainly meaningless office job or moving money from here to there or even the doctor's hopeless and endless effort to make a real dent in human suffering. And they talked about the inevitable stasis in marriages or, in other cases, the way that a divorced person can drift away from human contact until all that's left is a person and their reflection in the mirror. The shades asked, in voices that might have been designed to still the blood, *What is this life all* about? *What have you been working* for? *What do you suppose you can really* achieve? And everywhere throughout the haunted house — coming not just from the dark grandfather clock but the floors and walls and furniture, too — was the sound of ticking time.

Afterward, some of these people abruptly left the area, and their families, altogether. And always in the middle of the night between a Sunday and the oncoming workweek.

This should have been the end of it — the new and heavy silence in all our homes that held either teenagers or middle-aged parents should have convinced the rest of us to steer clear.

Of course it didn't.

## THE HAUNTING HOUSE

Young couples, pregnant or trying or with newborns keeping them up at night, crept next along the wobbly stone path to the haunted house. But they crept with marginally more confidence than the ones who came before, armored as they were in the brightness of their futures and armed with all kinds of plans for how to improve on the previous generation's feeble efforts. Take the Vaughn-Pitchers, who, hand in hand, actually approached the place with smiles — brittle, maybe, but smiles all the same — on their faces.

Still — when they came back out again, their drawn and foggy faces told the tale. The shades had vividly shown them the world they were handing their children, one considerably worse, even, than what was shown on the news, whether in terms of climate change or human conflict or a collapsing economy. And although that might certainly have been enough, the ghosts had also connected these young adults to their inner world, which was a landscape rich with arguments for why none of them had any business becoming parents.

The Vaughn-Pitchers were certainly not smiling when they left.

It might go without saying that the one liquor store on the edge of our suburb saw a tremendous uptick in business throughout this period.

Younger kids also braved the haunted house, when pushed by daring friends, when parents weren't watching. Stevie P., Emma A., Lucas L. All of them, in tense little groups. They, more than anyone else, seemed to know that they were in for something bad. And inside they heard about the mistakes of fathers and mothers, the dangers and obstacles they weren't really paying attention to. These kids learned a thing that they had always suspected: the ghosts explained the ways that parents had no idea what they were doing. The shades made them see that adults *in general* had no idea what they were doing. That there was nowhere, nowhere at all, to turn for help.

Finally: the elders among us? Although the front walk was very unsteady for them, although the unevenness of the porch steps was a significant barrier, they, too, made their way. They took their places in the cobwebbed loveseats and armchairs — old Mrs. Orson said that the chair she sat in seemed almost familiar, like something from her childhood — and they, too, listened to the shades. Who spoke, of course, of impending decay and death and being alone in the end. These ideas weren't new to many of the elders, which was why a lot of them were less altered by the experience than the rest of us. Old Mr. Grant said that he already had a version of the house inside him, pointed out that all of us probably had a version of the house inside us. Some of these folks were even somewhat at peace with what they'd heard. Though the word *alone* remained thereafter a sensitive one for every elder in the town.

By a certain point — probably late June — nearly everyone in the community had made a visit. You felt that fact in every living room, on every square of sidewalk. Although the early signs were that, thanks to the bats, it was indeed going to be a summer of fewer mosquitos, our neighborhood was clearly on wobbly footing.

And many of us were going back for second and third visits, and coming out worse every time. Like picking at a wound, somehow we couldn't help ourselves.

Something, in other words, needed to be done. There were those who argued that the only way past is *through* — the Hadleys were loudest here — and that we needed to face our demons in regular, repeated sessions in the house, but the demeanors of those who had already gone back made this plan seem naïve. Others, like both Drs. Mitchell, said that we needed to make it clearer to everyone that the property was *off-limits*, and maybe even to put up some modern fencing. Razor wire; electrification, perhaps. Unfortunately, none of us believed for a second that any of that would keep us out. We talked about exorcism, but even the modest religious diversity of our community made that idea awfully complicated. Meanwhile, the idea of complaining to the opaque corporation that had designed and built the house was laughable.

Dr. Ballinger suggested we burn the place to the ground, an idea that was surprisingly well-received until it was pointed out that we had *wanted* a haunted house, hadn't we? If we engaged in arson, we'd be losing our status symbol. Our gravitas, our suburb almost having a sense of history.

But we did have a library whose architecture was not uninteresting, and there was that spot a few blocks away where a semi-important painter once painted, long ago, before the meadow was cleared for homes. And some of the cars at our curbs were expensive. We did have status.

And so ultimately we all stood at the edge of the property, a neighborhood rallied to a single purpose. We had our gasoline and lighters; the young Vaughn-Pitcher couple and a few other people even assembled Molotov cocktails. The haunted house looked vulnerable, with its dried-out tall grass in the front lawn — it was July by then — and its decaying wood porch, its listing structure. It looked ready, maybe even *hungry*, to burn.

And so who can explain the way we stood there, unmoving, not one of us stepping forward to start the blaze? Were there shades at the windows, their voices in our heads issuing warnings?

In the end, it was decided for us. Mr. Taylor, spooked by a bat, threw his Molotov cocktail defensively, and although he hadn't lit the cloth sticking out of the bottle, something — could it have been the friction of it smashing on the porch? — started the fire going. Others, freed from their indecision, added their incendiaries to the flames.

And indeed the house went up quickly, as though it was made of kindling. Still unmoving, we watched the place disappear in the conflagration; we watched it burn to the ground. We stared at it all night until we were staring at embers. The grass was gone, too; everything aside from the fences had burned, and those had fallen — outward.

The one thing that we hadn't really considered, until now, was that burning a haunted house might free the spirits to roam the town at will. Had those warning shades at the windows been reminding us of something crucial: that preserving the house was the only hope we had to convince ourselves that our lives were ever, even briefly, different *outside* it?

It was too late for that consideration. The house — that terrible container — was broken and gone.

We dropped our remaining tools of destruction. We returned uncertainly to our homes. It was done. Certainly something had been done.

And now?

Now we live like this.

# THE MACABRE READER

## LYSETTE STEVENSON

**THE BLOODY COUNTESS: The Crimes of Erzsebet Bathory** *by Valentine Penrose, translated from French by Alexander Trocchi. Creation Books, 1996.*

At the time, Bathory was one of the most powerful families in Europe. Despite this, Penrose details how the family lineage was filled with inbreeding and mental illness. Most of Erzsebet's close relations committed suicide and Erzsebet herself showed early signs of psychopathic fixation. With the aid of servants who enabled and encouraged the Countess' bloodlust, she allegedly tortured and murdered 650 servant girls. Bathory wasn't reprimanded until she started taking victims from the upper classes under the guise that she was running a boarding school for ladies. The gravity of the crimes and body count of Erzsebet could easily be chalked up as hearsay, if it wasn't for the detailed journals the

Countess kept that sealed her fate. Erzsebet was bricked into a tower of her castle to live out her life in darkness and solitude.

While there are many histories written about this notorious mass murderer, Valentine Penrose makes an interesting biographer. Herself a poet and one of the first women of the Surrealist movement. With a passion for erotism and transgression, the subject of a female serial killer clearly fascinated her. Penrose's personal interest in the occult and alchemy fleshes out conclusions about Bathory's own knowledge of witchcraft. Despite the horrifying subject matter, Penrose's language is fiery and passionate. Vividly bringing to life the sado-masochism of Bathory and her wards. Further translated to English by poet and Situationist Alexander Trocchi, *The Bloody Countess* is a seductive and hallucinatory look into the darkness of wealth and power.

∼

**Let's Kill Uncle** *by Rohan O'Grady, pen name for June Skinner. Ace paperback, 1963.*

In *Let's Kill Uncle*, O'Grady creates a beguiling cast of characters, each with their own pathos and wonderfully blackish sense of humor. Set on a small island off the coast of British Columbia, life there is quiet until two scrappy city children arrive for their summer internment.

The strong-willed young girl was shipped off by her single mother to live with her surrogate aunt, dubbed the 'Goat Lady.' The precocious orphaned boy, heir to an enormous fortune, was sent to the island to be cared for by the doting spiritualists and proprietors of the general store. Until his military uncle arrives to take charge of him.

The boy dreads his uncle's arrival, claiming him to be a sadist and a werewolf, certain his uncle has plans to murder him for his inheritance. Meanwhile a rogue cougar is on the island after having killed an indigenous child on the mainland. In an act of magic realism the narrator takes us into the mind of the cougar as it hides and is reluctantly befriended by the children. While the children plot a murder in the village church and tend to the graves in the churchyard, the uncle is whistling in the woods as he digs two tiny plots. *Let's Kill Uncle* is a charmingly macabre horror thriller, as if David Lynch directed an episode of the *Beachcombers* or *Northern Exposure*.

**They: A Sequence of Unease** by Kay Dick. First published Penguin Books, 1977. Reprinted 2022, Alfred A. Knopf Canada.

*They* is set in the 1970's, in the pastoral coastal countryside of England. The story is revealed more in what it doesn't tell you than what it does. Neighbors are subdued yet cheerful. There is a sense of restraint and propriety. Looming in the background are alien-like beings, keeping watch over the neighborhoods and it is implied that other counties have it worse. Everyone keeps busy with creative projects yet there is a constant threat that if they fail to stay the course, everything, including their memories, will be wiped from them. This reality is accepted and resistance to it is muted. As a reader you might be witnessing the last village that hasn't been taken over by this invading force. The measured rise in horror is wholly unnerving and still reads fresh as if it was written in modern day.

Much of the novella could be read as a metaphor for Kay Dick's own life as a queer woman, choosing a path against the norms of British society: childless, in polyamorous relationships, and pursuing a creative life rather than one of the wife and mother. A lost novel for decades with the pocket book scarce and out of print. It was said Kay Dick tried to get the rights back from Penguin who, possibly out of

*THE MACABRE READER*

spite for the novella selling poorly, persistently refused her request. Kay Dick passed away in 2001.

∼

**Arctic Dreams and Nightmares**
*written & illustrated by Alootook Ipellie. Theytus Books, 1993.*

Alootook Ipellie was born and raised in Iqaluit, to a family still living a traditional nomadic lifestyle in the world's most inhospitable climate. They developed mythologies, demigods and a way of storytelling unique to the Inuit. Alootook came of age as the Canadian government was allocating reserves and relocating children to residential schools. He moved to southern Ontario to integrate into this new society, later establishing himself as an Inuit artist. His work, often horrific, sexually explicit, and black with humor, was too shocking for the establishment's idea of what Inuit Art was.

In the early 1990's indigenous publisher Theytus Books encouraged Alootook Ipellie to write stories from a series of his more explicit illustrations. With twenty pen and ink drawings Alootook envisions shamans journeying between worlds. Stories encountering gods on dog sleds and otherworldly beasts. Of adulterous wives and demon exorcisms. In another, the media swarm for photos of Brigette Bardot as she protests traditional hunting. Monstrous polar bears, tundra wolves, ballerina walruses, and whale bone crucifixions. Gorgons and blues bands playing under the northern celestial skies. Pulling from traditional folklore passed down through generations, intermingling Christian iconography and his people's cultural genocide. With as much humor as horror, Alootook's collection of illustrative tales takes you into a world few people could ever experience or imagine.

∼

**Vampiro: The Vampire Bat in Fact and Fantasy** *by David E. Brown. University of Utah Press, 1999.*

David E. Brown wrote *Vampiro* with the layman biologist in mind. Stories from the trials and tribulations of field trips to the native habitats of vampire bats in Mexico, South America, and the Caribbean are written in a light and engaging manner. Entering the bat caves, crawling with insects who feed on the guano slurry of rotting blood beneath the roosts, Brown details the bats precarious life and their need to feed daily or else starve to death. How the bats will adopt orphans and care for weaker and older members of the colony by regurgitating blood is written quite endearingly. When it reached the chapter on efforts to control bats due to their spread of rabies amongst the cattle, I couldn't help but side with the bats and was horrified by the farmers' methods.

The idea that vampire bats exist in Eastern Europe is a misnomer. The term 'Vampire' was applied to this bat species because of the long-established European folklore for blood drinkers. The salacious appetite the European public had for the explorations of this mysterious New World helped validate long held beliefs in the supernatural.

In the latter half of the book Brown does a thorough cinephile history of bloodsuckers in media and pop culture, broadening *Vampiro* to a must read for Chiroptera aficionados or vampire enthusiasts in general.

∼

**Weird Ways of Witchcraft** *by Dr. Leo L. Martello. Castle Books, 1973.*

Dr. Leo Martello was a gay rights pioneer, feminist, animal rights activist, and practicing witch, at the forefront of the Neo-Pagan movement in the 1960's. Organizing protests and happenings for the New York based Gay Liberation Front and founding the Witches

## THE MACABRE READER

Anti-Defamation League, he was a prolific writer, publisher, and activist for most of his life.

Condemnation of the church is a running theme throughout the book. Leo gives a personal account of his negative experience in a Catholic boarding school and his initiation into Sicilian witchcraft. He shares a manifesto against the church and their history of persecutions, demanding $500 million in reparations for the inquisition against witches and a further $100 million for the descendants of the Salem witch trials. He argues that gender fluidity existed amongst magic practitioners throughout history before the advent of Christian missionaries.

With sensational newspaper clippings and candid interviews, he touches on the history of witchcraft and necromancy throughout the world. From African Voudon to Bornean Dayaks and the use of occult practices in warfare. Descriptions of Black Mass's and Satanic Oaths, to common folk hexes. He packs a lot in, it's a chaotic melting pot of Egyptian rituals, Masonic lodges, and indigenous shamans. Heavily illustrated with iconography and traditional woodcuts, the *Weird Ways of Witchcraft* is a veritable scrapbook of Witchery from the hippie era.

∽

**Tear** *by Erica McKeen. Cover design Megan Fildes. Invisible Books, 2022.*

A debut novel by Canadian writer Erica McKeen. McKeen explores how inherited trauma shapes the stories we tell ourselves and the ways it haunts our lives. Told in three parts with different narrators, much like the ambiguity of its title, the novel keeps you guessing what is real and what is imagined.

McKeen introduces us to a reclusive university student, Frances, living in a co-housing basement suite. When Frances suddenly finds herself trapped in the basement with no way of escape she loses all sense of time. Hunger mixed with insomnia foment nightmares, while figments of her imagination occupy the dank basement. She flits from memories of her childhood being raised by her grandparents and her grandfather's penchant for a spooky tale. To her friendship with a troublesome neighborhood boy, the disintegration of her parents' marriage, and the inheritance of mental illness. In her delirium the house begins speaking to her, demanding she adhere to ritual and order. Frances becomes the ultimate unreliable narrator. Is she dreaming? Is she living inside her grandfather's stories? Is there something larger than a rat scratching behind her bedroom wall? As her roommates upstairs take little interest in her absence and leave her to her own demise, a homunculus in this haunted house takes form.

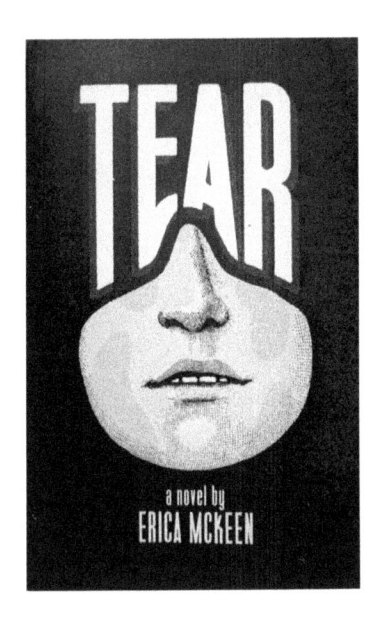

Charlotte Perkins Gilman, Mary Shelley, and Shirley Jackson blazed the trail of literary horror from the female psyche. McKeen brings to this a fresh, disorienting and claustrophobic narrative, filled with gut churning tension and body horror. A ghoulish and harrowing suburban gothic.

# CONTRIBUTORS

**David Ebenbach** is the author of nine books of fiction, poetry, and non-fiction, including his recent (and weird) novel *How to Mars*. He lives with his family in Washington, DC, where he teaches creative writing and literature and works with faculty and graduate students on their teaching, all at Georgetown University. You can find out more at davidebenbach.com.

**Orrin Grey** is a skeleton who likes monsters as well as the author of several spooky books. His stories of ghosts, monsters, and sometimes the ghosts of monsters can be found in dozens of anthologies, including Ellen Datlow's *Best Horror of the Year*. He resides in the suburbs of Kansas City and watches lots of scary movies. You can visit him online at orringrey.com.

**Vince Haig** is an illustrator, designer, and author. You can visit Vince at his website: barquing.com

**John Patrick Higgins** is a writer, illustrator and filmmaker. His short fiction has been published in the anthology *The Black Dreams*, two editions of *The BHF Book of Horror Stories*, and four editions of *Exacting Clam*. He is working on a book of short stories called *The Devil in Music*. His story *The Wink and the Gun* will be published in

## CONTRIBUTORS

the forthcoming *Fears: An Anthology of Psychological Terror* by Tachyon. His debut novel, *Fine*, will be published by *Sagging Meniscus Press* in 2024, and the same company will be publishing his essay, *Teeth: An Oral History*. His first film, *Goat Songs*, premiered at the 2021 Belfast Film Festival. His second, *Muirgen*, premiered at the *Paracinema Cult Film Festival* in 2023. He currently has two feature films languishing in development heaven. He lives in Belfast, goes for long walks in the rain, and sings in the post rock band, *Ebbing House*.

**James Hutton** is an artist/illustrator based in rural England. Working mainly in pen and ink, pencil and charcoal on paper, his artwork is often based around themes of rapacious consumerism, greed, poverty, nature and some random things, which then get put through a mangler of disparate inspirations — among them medieval and outsider art, folklore, the horror movie posters of the 1970s and 80s, politics and punk rock! Visit him at: jameshuttonillustration.com

**Jack Klausner** lives in the U.K. His short fiction has appeared in *The Dark, ergot, hex*, and elsewhere. You can find him at jackklausner.com or on Bluesky @jackklausner

**Jess Koch** is a writer, software engineer, and graduate of the Stonecoast MFA program. Her work has been published in many places including *Bourbon Penn, Fusion Fragment*, and the Bram Stoker Award-nominated anthology, *Chromophobia*. Jess grew up on an island off the coast of Maine and now lives in a pre-civil war colonial somewhere in New England with her partner, dog, and probably a few ghosts. She is currently working on a novel. You can find her online at jesskoch.com

**Gary McMahon** is the author of the "Thomas Usher" novels, *The Concrete Grove* trilogy, *The Bones of You*, and several short story collections. His short fiction has been reprinted in various "Year's Best" anthologies. A feature film adaptation of his award-nominated novella *The Grieving Stones* is currently shooting in the U.K. and Guernsey. Gary lives, works and writes in Yorkshire, where he lives with his wife, son, and two meddlesome felines.

# CONTRIBUTORS

**Jacob Steven Mohr** does not believe in human consciousness; his works emerge as though from the ether, fully formed and fully ominous. Selections of these can be observed in *Cosmic Horror Monthly, Shortwave Magazine, Chthonic Matter Quarterly,* and *The Best Horror of the Year, Vol. 15*. He exists in Columbus OH. Follow him everywhere @jacobstevenmohr.

**Alison Moore's** short stories have been included in *Best British Short Stories* and *Best British Horror* and broadcast on BBC Radio. They have been collected in *The Pre-War House and Other Stories* and *Eastmouth and Other Stories*. Her debut novel, *The Lighthouse*, was shortlisted for the Man Booker Prize and the National Book Awards, winning the McKitterick Prize. She recently published her fifth novel, *The Retreat*, and a trilogy for children, beginning with *Sunny and the Ghosts*.

**Aimee Ogden** is an American werewolf in the Netherlands. Her debut novella, *Sun-Daughters, Sea-Daughters*, was a Nebula Award Finalist, and her most recent novella, *Emergent Properties*, arrived in July 2023. Her short fiction has appeared in publications such as *Lightspeed, Clarkesworld,* and *Strange Horizons*, and she also co-edits *Translunar Travelers Lounge*, a magazine of fun and optimistic speculative fiction.

**Elin Olausson** is a fan of the weird and the unsettling. She is the author of the short story collections *Growth* and *Shadow Paths* and has had stories featured in *34 Orchard, Chiral Mad 5, Nightscript,* and many other publications. Elin's rural childhood made her love and fear the woods, and she firmly believes that a cat is your best companion in life. She lives in Sweden.

**Perry Ruhland** is a writer based in Chicago. His writing has previously been published in *Baffling Magazine, The Cafe Irreal, Vastarien Magazine, Chthonic Matter Quarterly,* and *ergot*. Learn more at perryruhland.com

**Lysette Stevenson** is a stage manager with a rural outdoor equestrian theatre company and a second generation bookseller. She lives in British Columbia.

## CONTRIBUTORS

**Simon Strantzas** is the author of five collections of short fiction, including *Only the Living Are Lost* (Hippocampus Press, 2023), and editor of a number of anthologies, including *Year's Best Weird Fiction, Vol. 3*. Combined, he's been a finalist for four Shirley Jackson Awards, two British Fantasy Awards, and the World Fantasy Award. His fiction has appeared in numerous annual best-of anthologies, and in venues such as *Nightmare*, *The Dark*, and *Cemetery Dance*. In 2014, his edited anthology, *Aickman's Heirs*, won the Shirley Jackson Award. He lives with his wife in Toronto, Canada.

**RJ Taylor** is a queer speculative fiction writer based outside Boston. She's a member of the Codex writer's group and a recent graduate of Viable Paradise. Her short fiction has appeared in *Factor Four, Apex Magazine, The Magazine of Fantasy & Science Fiction*, and *Clarkesworld*.